2035

DEREK LEABERRY

PAGE PUBLISHING
Conneaut Lake, PA

First originally published by Page Publishing 2022

ISBN 978-1-6624-8801-6 (pbk)
ISBN 978-1-6624-8800-9 (digital)

Printed in the United States of America

The man slipped out of his dream, heard the pitter-patter of light rain, and felt the cool on his face from the breeze outside the open window. He felt exhilarated by the wet, cool air. His eyes opened, and he sat up and looked out the open window. Dawn was beginning, but the sun was still on the other side of the mountain and would be for a little while longer. He could hear the river whispering lightly in the distance a quarter mile from the house. Looking out the window, he could see puffs of cloud hovering seventy-five feet above the river along its length for as far as the man could see. Overhead, he heard an airliner as it began its descent to the airport fifty miles to the east, a modern infringement on the natural world of the mountains, river, and farm.

As he always did at this time in the morning, Roger kicked his legs out from the bed, and his feet landed on the wood floor of the bedroom. As he pulled on his blue jeans, he heard a diesel downshifting two miles away as it slowed into the town in the small valley. Next, Roger pulled on his red-and-green checkered flannel shirt and buttoned it. He grabbed a pair of white socks and his shoes and walked off to the kitchen to brew a pot of coffee.

It was Saturday, and Roger would not be cooking his own breakfast. He rarely cooked breakfast on Saturdays, preferring to eat at Mike's Diner in the town. He liked eating out for Saturday breakfast and had done so for many years because it allowed him to be among friends he had known all his life. Saturday breakfast was much more than bacon and eggs eaten out.

Mike's Diner was located on the main street of Stonewall. Stonewall was really nothing more than a village, home to no more than three hundred people. Stonewall didn't have a traffic light, and the only traffic light in the county was over twenty miles away at the courthouse. The firehouse was Stonewall's central building, across the street from the funeral home. A convenience store sold gas, beer, tobacco, lottery tickets, and a few groceries. Young women made sandwiches at a counter toward the left side of the front entrance. There was a long bench outside the store for the men to congregate and talk. It was called the Liar's Bench by the men.

Attached to the convenience store was a small hardware store owned by Roger's old high school football teammate, Zack Johnson. Roger and Zack were the high school outside linebackers almost forty years in the past. Zack's father ran the hardware store before him, and Zack's grandfather ran it before Zack's father. Almost everyone in Stonewall went to the Johnson hardware store as it was the only hardware within a fifteen-minute drive. The drive wasn't worth the dollar you saved on a box of nails.

Stonewall had a Family Dollar and a Dollar General at opposite ends of town. Stonewall was too small to support a chain supermarket. If a wife needed a gravy enhancer at the last moment, she drove to one of the two chain convenience stores. If a kid wanted chips or sodas or candy bars, he rode his bike down to the Family Dollar or the Dollar General. Stores like Family Dollar and Dollar General filled a need for the people of Stonewall that city folk or suburbanites wouldn't understand.

A struggling Mexican restaurant that served poor food sat at the south edge of town next door to Val's barbershop. In a strip of stores was an Italian takeaway, Dr. Osborne's dental office, Sam's small engine-repair shop, and a Laundromat. The stores were built about ten years before, comparatively new buildings for Stonewall. They had aged poorly and looked weather-beaten and not maintained. Two small banks faced each other, small-blocked buildings fitting for a town the size of Stonewall. There was one boarded-up building, Richardson's Gun Shop. Richardson's had been in business for many years, but it closed five years ago when the national government outlawed handguns. It was rumored that Yancey Richardson sold hand-

guns on the black market, but Richardson wasn't big enough for the government to crack down on.

In the actual town limits of Stonewall, almost all the residential homes dated from the days before World War I. Many were big with front porches. Some were made of brick or stone or masonry. They all looked solid and individually made and not slapped up like suburban houses far away or some of the newer houses outside of Stonewall built on sold-off farms and made into mini-developments. The newer houses had been slapped up cheaply and looked it. These houses aged poorly because they were built solely for profit. The older houses had been handcrafted and built as homes for families.

Roger drove his black Ford truck down the dirt road, raising dust in his wake. A doe and her two fawns walked the dewy morning grass that was part of the neighboring Bradshaw farm. The doe looked up at the truck, jumped a fence, and ran to some woodlands at the far edge of the Bradshaw farm. The fawns scampered about in fear but were too young to jump the fence. Their panic subsided as Roger continued up the dirt road.

Mike's Diner was small because in a town Stonewall's size there wasn't a need for a large building. About a dozen tables sat about the dining area. Most of the tables were along the windows that dominated three sides of Mike's. The fourth side was the kitchen, open as the diners could watch the cooks cooking the food. The tables sat four people except for the long table at the center of the room where regular diners preferred to sit with other diners whom they had known for decades. Most of Mike's diners knew each other and had known each other for many years.

"Hello, Roger," called out an old bearded man with long gray hair and wearing suspenders of faded jean. The man forked a solid home-fried potato, dipped it into a bit of egg yolk, and ate. The man ate at the far end of the long table where he usually did.

"Good morning, Zeb," answered Roger Lee as he walked over and sat alone at a table near a window. "How you been, Zeb? A little wet today. Going to cut hay or not?"

"No. Too wet. Gonna take today off. No reason to fight the wet. Dry next week probably. I suppose I'll hay next week," replied Zeb.

A ruddy-faced, stout man of about sixty wearing a dirty John Deere baseball cap called out to Zeb from a corner table. "Got to hate the rain when you need to hay. The weather never fits a man's hay-cutting schedule. But it could be worse. Rain is slacking already, and I bet we get a little sun before the end of the day. I bet you'll be able to cut hay by Monday."

The ruddy-faced man was Jerry Blanchard, and he had a farm a mile outside the actual town. Jerry was one of Stonewall's leading citizens. He kept over one hundred head of cattle and grew potatoes, corn, tomatoes, and greens. He was a builder as well. Mike's had been built by Jerry's construction company as had been the Mexican restaurant and the strip of stores. So was the Stonewall Bank, of which Jerry was on the board of directors. Some of the newer houses outside the town had been built by Jerry Blanchard and his building company.

Eating beside Jerry was his son, Steve, who wore his dark hair close-cropped. Steve was tall and well-built and had been a linebacker for the county football team a decade ago. Both muscular forearms were tattooed with barbed wire. He had served a hitch in the Marines and had used his Marine money to go to realtor school when his tour was completed. He who knows the price of land makes money. Steve had learned most of what he knew about land from his father, who had been dealing in land for decades. But the school learning and diploma came in handy.

Waffle McCall, Jerry's sister's youngest boy, sat across from his cousin. Waffle, who preferred pancakes to waffles, was eating voraciously a large piece of country ham, which he mopped with orange egg yolk. Nobody in Stonewall knew why Waffle was given the name Waffle, but nobody questioned why. It just was. Waffle was a big man in his early twenties, beefy with an uncombed forest of dark brown hair covered by a Pittsburgh Pirates baseball cap. Waffle was sloppy where Steve was disciplined, but they were kin, and they fished and hunted together and had done so since they were boys. Waffle had only started working for his uncle as a carpenter's assistant.

A waitress walked over toward Roger from the small counter separating the dining room from the kitchen. Her name was Carlyn.

Young and unmarried, she was eight months pregnant. Carlyn lived alone in a trailer three miles east of Stonewall. She kept her brown hair long, and it reached to the middle of her back. She was short and a little dumpy and wore a tattoo of a rose on her left arm. Her pregnancy forced her to waddle to Roger's table with a menu in one hand and a cup of black coffee in the other. Roger always drank his coffee black.

"Hello, Mr. Lee," she said as she came up to the table.

"Hi, Carlyn. How are you doing?" Roger smiled as Carlyn set down the menu and coffee. "And call me Roger, Carlyn. You make me feel old when you pull that *mister* stuff."

"I know, I know," Carlyn replied. "How are you getting along?"

"It's been two months, and I'm still getting used to Connie not being around. It is hard to believe she's gone. Thirty-three years of marriage. Connie taught your parents and a lot of other people in this room."

"Everybody loved Mrs. Lee. Miss Connie."

"That's right. Me too." He paused. "Thanks for your kindness, Carlyn. She loved her students, and she loved this town and this county."

Carlyn walked away and Roger glanced at the menu, but he pretty much knew what he wanted—two eggs over easy, sausage patties, and home fries. He drank some coffee, and Carlyn came back to take his order. He stuck with what he usually had on Saturday morning at Mike's.

Jimmy Sirbaugh came into Mike's through one of the side doors. He was sturdy, about forty years old, and wore his graying red hair long. His face was weathered and lined, and he wore a red beard, which contrasted with his bright blue eyes. He wore a dirty yellow cap, and his forearms were tattooed, a red bull on one arm and a comet on the other. Jimmy was a plumber just like his father. Sirbaugh Plumbing was the biggest plumbing company in the county.

"Hi, Uncle Bob," Jimmy Sirbaugh called out. He strode to the table Bob Strong was eating at closer to the counter and sat down next to the old man. Bob was Jimmy's mother's older brother. "What do you know, Uncle Bob?"

Bob smiled, slapped his nephew on his right arm, and replied, "Well, I know I ain't cutting hay today, that's for sure. Too damned wet." Bob Strong looked over to Zeb Holliday and called out, "Hey, Zeb, are you cutting today?"

"No way," answered Zeb Holliday. "This ain't a day to hay in, for sure."

"You know it," said Jimmy Sirbaugh. "What ya gonna do with yourself today, Uncle Bob?"

"Pick the rest of the tomatoes with Loretta and help her jar 'em up, I suppose."

Carlyn came up to the table with coffee, a small container of cream, and two packs of sugar. She slid the coffee in front of Jimmy.

"You eating here or at your own table?" Carlyn asked.

Uncle Bob answered, "Put Jimmy on my tab, but don't eat the whole house, Jimmy. Carlyn, bring me some more coffee, dear."

Shane Batson and Barry Doggle walked into Mike's. Shane was tall and lean and in his late twenties, and he wore a large cowboy hat that John Wayne would have been proud to wear. He wore sideburns and a mustache. Barry was a smaller man of about the same age, and he wore shorts and a colorful polo shirt. He carried his iPhone in his right hand. The two young men walked to an open table toward the back of the room.

"Where you think you are, Barry?" called out Zeb. "You think this is Hawaii or something? Ya think you're at the beach." Zeb chuckled.

"I'm doin' all right, Zeb. You like these shorts, don't ya? Good looking on me, right?"

"You workin' in them shorts?" asked Zeb.

"Yeah, I am."

"A bit cool out there for shorts," said Zeb.

"No matter," replied Barry, and he began fidgeting with his iPhone.

A middle-aged couple with a young boy and a young girl came into Mike's. They sat the two children down at the last open table near the center of the restaurant, and the two of them walked over to Roger's table. Wil Yeager was a slender, dark-haired man in his midfifties and wore black slacks and a polo shirt that was upscale for Mike's. Wil was president of the Stonewall Bank. Brenda was his wife, chunky with blond hair that curled below her neck and bounced when she walked. She was the only woman in Mike's who wore a dress. It was colored mauve with yellow daisies and hung below her knees.

Wil pulled out a chair for Brenda and then sat down himself.

"You doing all right?" Wil asked.

"Yeah, I'm doing fine. I'm not used to cooking for one. I have a lot of leftovers. If I cook a pot of spaghetti, I have a week's worth of food. Or so it seems. It can lead to monotonous eating."

"We'd like to have you come over soon for some supper," said Brenda. She cupped her hands together and smiled. "You just name the day."

"You know, I'm partial to your roast beef and mashed potatoes and dark gravy. Fine eating, Brenda. I've really liked your beef stroganoff in the past too."

"Yeah, Brenda can cook some," said Wil.

"She sure can. I haven't eaten better food than when it comes from Brenda's kitchen. Delicious food, that's for sure," said Roger.

Wil looked at Roger with squinty eyes and smiled broadly. "Roger, when do you plan to finish harvesting the rest of your crop?"

"Soon," answered Roger. "Maybe two weeks. Not any more than that. It's time. Pretty close to time to get the apples picked and sold off. It'll be November before you know it. Really looking forward to harvesting the apples, so I can fish some this fall and hunt later on."

"Good for you," Brenda replied. "You need time off. Time to put the bad times behind you. Connie was such a sweet woman, loved by everybody. Everybody."

"Thanks," said Roger.

"She's missed, Roger," said Wil. He paused. "Keep in touch. Come by the bank anytime or the house, ya hear?"

"I will."

The Yeagers got up and went back to their own table to order for themselves and their grandchildren. Mike's was full now, and people were eating their simple food, enjoying each other's company, chattering back and forth between the several tables. They were friends.

Carlyn brought Roger his food. The eggs were fresh and oozed a striking bright orange so different from the yolk of industrialized eggs. Yolk ran to the sausage patties at the center of the plate. Roger cut off a piece of sausage, soaked it into the yolk, and ate. Delicious. He forked a piece of potato and dabbed it into the yolk and ate that. Very good.

Roger finished his food ten minutes later. Roger's coffee was topped by Carlyn, and he looked over the room. He noticed Bill Dunwood eating a pancake drenched with sausage gravy, a popular meal at Mike's. His wife, Mary Lou, ate an omelet. Dunwood worked for the state highway administration and was part of a crew that cut back the many trees that threatened to fall onto the roads. In the mountains, downed trees could tie up roads for long periods, so it was important to cut them down or pare them back ahead of time. Mary Lou taught the third grade at the elementary school a half mile outside of Stonewall.

Wil Yeager finished his breakfast and walked over to Roger's table and sat. He asked, "Roger, why does the government leave us alone?" Wil drummed the table lightly with his right hand.

"We're not a threat to them, Wil. We're not worth spending energy and resources on. The government has plenty on its plate, and we're not worth the time. We mean nothing to the national government. We're not even really a nuisance. We're an anachronism. Just a bunch of country bumpkins just getting by."

"Not important enough to crack down on."

"That's right," replied Roger. "We're isolated in our mountains and in our ranches and farms and small towns and small houses and small businesses. Most people up our way live in a different century."

"A better century, don't you think?"

"In most ways. Of course, the twenty-first century hasn't had two world wars. As bad as are the politicians today, there's no aspiring Hitler or Stalin or Mao or Lenin. Most of the countries get along. Food is plentiful. You can buy virtually anything on the internet you might want. Books, clothes, machines, gadgets, houses, cars, pornography." Roger smiled. "Of course, manners and morals are shot to hell. Millions of small businesses have been rubbed out by the internet. Widespread atomization of society has replaced neighborliness and community. Who needs a diner like Mike's when you can carry out food and eat alone at home while you watch TV or fool around on your computer or iPhone? But I am preaching."

"Do you get worried that the authorities will come up in the mountains and crack down on us sometime down the road?" Will asked with a frown. "You know, like they've done in the cities."

"Could be. Somewhere down the line. Maybe when I'm dead," said Roger and he grinned. "The good thing about living on mountain land that has no coal is that we have no value to people who run things these days."

"They cracked down on our handguns. Put Yancey Richardson out of business. I still hold the note on his building."

"That they did. The symbolism of an independent man with a handgun was too much for the national government. So they banned the handgun after the courts declared the Second Amendment null and void. No longer relevant to a modern society. Used the Fourteenth Amendment to get rid of the Second, so the Second was flushed down the toilet. Of course, the cities are filled with handgun killings just like twenty years ago or fifty years ago. And I can't remember the last time anyone in this county has been killed by a handgun. Doesn't make sense."

"The television never reports crime anymore," replied Wil. "Nowadays you only hear about city crime by rumor or word of mouth. I think the government tells the television and radio stations to hold off reporting crime stories. It is plain racist to mention crime and who is killing who."

"Even when we were much younger, Wil, there was a revolving door between the national government and the networks. Incestuous." Wil Yeager nodded.

"Got to get going, Roger. Good talking to you," said Wil.

"Good to talk to you, Wil," Roger replied. "Time for me to get."

Roger paid the check and left three dollar bills on his table and left Mike's. The rain had stopped. A Stonewall police car pulled into the parking lot, and Roger gathered it was Mac Thomas, the police chief of the four-man town police force. Mac stepped out of the cruiser and walked toward Mike's for breakfast.

Mac was a medium-sized man whose graying hair was a crew cut. He had a stern oval face, and his eyes were black. Mac had served in the Army during the first Iraq War, returned home, and eventually became a town cop. He had been the chief for over a decade.

"How are you, Roger?" Mac asked with a smile.

"Doing fine, Mac. A little stuffed with food. I need to work a little bit of it off. Maybe I'll pick apples. Maybe I'll fish. What's new with you?"

"Some bureaucrat with the national government is circulating the idea of registration of long guns. Can you imagine?" Mac shook his head, rolled his eyes, and smiled broadly. "Can you imagine anyone up here registering their rifles and shotguns? Incredible. Nobody in our county turned in a handgun when the government banned them and offered a bounty to turn them in. Only a government worker in the city could come up with a scheme to register long guns."

"Would they want you to enforce it? How could you? And think about jurisdiction. Most of us don't live in the actual town of Stonewall. All the hunting grounds are outside of town."

"Yeah, I guess they'd ask the Sheriff's Department to enforce it. Of course, everyone in the Sheriff's Department owns rifles and shotguns, has family members who own long guns, and have good friends who own rifles and shotguns. Virtually everyone in the mountains owns a long gun of some sort."

"Unenforceable law, I suppose," replied Roger. "But if they pass such a law, that would make most people in the mountains into criminals."

"You ever think that's the idea, Roger?"

"Could very well be. When the national government has the ability to declare anyone a criminal, you have something like what happened in Stalin's Russia or Hitler's Germany. I hope it doesn't come to that."

"You never know," answered Mac with a shake of his head.

The two men parted, and Roger climbed into his truck and drove home.

Roger's farm was a little over sixty acres. Most of it was rolling hill and good grazing land. About ten acres was flatter, and here Roger kept about a hundred apple trees and a small grove of peach trees. He also kept a large garden of tomatoes, green peppers, hot peppers, cucumbers, and sweet corn. The garden was fenced ten feet into the sky to keep the deer out. Close by the house, Roger kept six raised beds for the smaller vegetables. The raised beds had been Connie's idea.

His house was made of brick and had been built by a wealthy family after the War Between the States. It was roomy with five bedrooms, a large kitchen with a table, a substantial dining room, and a large living room. Connie had kept a simple house. The dining room table was solid and could sit ten but was unadorned. In the living room, chairs and a sofa shared space with shelves of books. A small television sat on a console at one side of the room. Roger and Connie rarely watched the television.

A large barn built by Germans in the 1840s was a minute's walk away. It was larger than the house, over one hundred feet long and fifty wide. Its base was made of stone and the rest was wood, weathered gray-brown slats with small gaps between each board. The roof was a sun-and-rain beaten red and made of tin. The barn had two floors and a small loft. Two dozen laying chickens were kept in one pen in the lower barn. The pen emptied into a small fenced-in field, and the hens were allowed to roam the field during the day. Roger didn't keep roosters and hated them, preferring to buy hens by mail order to restock his hennery. Another pen housed the sheep. Roger kept four sheep for breeding purposes and had the rest butchered or sold each year. Roger and Connie loved to eat lamb, especially with Connie's homemade mint sauce. The lower barn also had four freezers filled with meat—beef, chicken, lamb, pork and venison. A half-dozen wooden cabinets contained vegetables, fruits, and jams preserved in glass Mason jars. In a small nook at the foot of the stairs was Roger's fishing gear.

Roger kept farm implements in the upper barn. The Kubota tractor was solid, and he could attach a disc harrow, a tedder, a rake, a rototiller, a baler, or even a grass mower to the back. But he kept a zero-turn Toro to cut what lawn he wanted cut. He kept a beat-up Cub Cadet that was thirty years old as a spare and a cheap Craftsman push mower that he hadn't used since the days when he had no gray hair. Roger hated to throw out equipment that worked even if it was never used.

Arriving home, Roger was restless and decided to visit a few of the farm stands that he sold apples to. He grabbed four bushels of apples in their wooden baskets and placed them in the back of the truck. He next grabbed a scuffed-up blue-and-white travel cooler, placed a half-dozen beers inside, and filled the cooler with a generous amount of ice. He placed the cooler in the back seat and took off down the road, kicking up gravel as he picked up speed. Two minutes later, Roger was driving through a canopy of green trees and slate-gray rocks.

Annie's Farm Stand was four miles away down a winding road from Stonewall near the smaller town of Benton's Corner. The road was all up and down, right curve then left curve, heavily forested with occasional grazing land with cattle and sometimes sheep. The houses were simple and old, and several were abandoned to dry rot. Roger often wondered how it came to be that a house was left to die. It had been new at one time and a family had lived there and had good times and sometimes bad times. Did some catastrophe happen? Or did the house deteriorate as the owners got old and the children went away to live their lives far away? Just like Roger's children. All four were gone and out of state, and one of them living in Seattle didn't bother to attend their mother's funeral and instead sent flowers.

Roger angled the truck at an incline sloping steep and blind near a large growth of woods and declined just as fast down what would have been a valley, but it didn't remain flat, and Roger was driving once again on an incline. The incline topped off, and fencing began, and it was the McNally place. About thirty head of cattle grazed in a sweet green pasture. A couple dozen rolls of brownish-yellow hay lay about the McNally farm. Brent McNally had hayed his land a month ago.

The road cut over a small bridge spanning Miller Creek and swerved left. The road flattened for about fifty yards. A doe shot across the road, and Roger braked and let the deer pass in front of him. It would be rut season in about a month. The bucks remained deep in the woods, and Roger couldn't remember the last time he saw a buck.

Roger banked the truck up another slope that rose fifty feet in the air, and the road cut again to the left. He left the woods behind, and the farm ahead on his right was a substantial farm with a farm silo, a large barn, and a large white Victorian house where the Wessinger family had owned land for over two centuries. Sam Wessinger ran over fifty cattle and a half-dozen buffalo on his two-hundred-acre spread. Sam kept twenty acres of his farm in corn, one of the few county farmers who kept so much acreage in corn. The corn had been harvested, and the dead stalks were brown. It would be made into feed before long.

Roger pulled off the road and drove up the hundred-yard driveway. Sam was at the barn. Sam and he had gone to high school together, double-dated together in school, and drank their first beer at sixteen together. Roger hadn't spoken with Sam for a few weeks and was in the mood to talk to one of his best friends. Roger took a quick sip of beer, put his plastic travel cup in the console cupholder, and got out of his truck.

"Hello, stranger," called out Sam from the entry of the barn. Sam was a big man with a block of a head, and he wore a long beard that was half gray. He wore blue-jean suspenders with a red sweatshirt underneath. The clothes had dirt stains and a few rips that were the sign of a man who worked with his hands.

"Mighty fine day, Sam, now that the rain has gone," said Roger as he walked over to the barn. The two men shook hands. Sam's right hand was strong and meaty and was missing part of his pinky.

"Better think that we should appreciate this fine weather. It'll get cold soon enough."

"Fall's a fine time of the year."

"Beats winter."

"Anything beats winter."

"What you out and about for?" asked Sam.

"See a few of the stands and see who wants more apples. Season finishing up. To be honest, I really wanted to get out and about. I feel a little restless. And I felt like knocking down a beer or two on a fall Saturday. Beats television."

"Do you watch it much?"

"No."

"Neither do I." Sam smiled. "Guess that makes me a misfit. A social undesirable."

"Me too. Deplorable, like someone once said a few years ago." Roger kicked at the dirt. "Want a beer?"

"Who wouldn't want a beer on a day like today? Yeah, time to knock off for the day. Let's go up to the porch and sit a while."

Roger went back to the truck and grabbed his unfinished beer from the truck and grabbed two fresh cold ones. The glass was icy and stung Roger's hands, but he was fine with that. He loved the feel of a bottle of cold beer.

The two men sat on unpainted wood chairs on the porch. A small wood table sat between the two chairs where the two men could place their beers.

"How's Becca?" Roger asked.

"Fine. She's canning apple-pie filling right now in the kitchen."

"Bet it smells great."

"Sure it does. And eats good too."

"There's nothing like a hot slice of apple pie with a scoop of vanilla ice cream on the side."

"That's a great sentiment. I heartily agree. Peach cobbler too."

"Yeah. And add blueberry pie. Even if you have to get the blueberries from North Carolina or Maine."

A little tensed, Roger asked, "How's Grif doing?"

"Much better, Roger. He's out of rehab." Sam drank a large mouthful of beer.

"What, was he in for a couple months?"

"Six weeks at a clinic in Ohio."

"The way the drug companies push their meds is a damned shame." Both men shook their heads.

"Sure enough. The drug companies got to make money too."

"Yeah, even if they have to screw millions of kids' lives up."

"You wonder how they can live with themselves."

"We are the overprescribed," answered Roger, and he slapped his right arm with his left. "Yeah, it is better to live in a world of medicine and antibiotics instead of the world of leeches, bleeding snake-oil salesmen, and charms. But the pill companies and their agents, the doctors, and the drugstores, especially the national-chain drugstores, hand out prescriptions like candy bars. Rotten. Damned rotten."

"It's a crazy old world."

"Ain't that true."

"Could you use another beer?" asked Sam. He stood and walked toward the open front door.

"Good idea. Don't mind if I do," answered Roger.

Sam came back with two cans of very cold beer. Little streams of water rimmed the cans top to bottom. Sam handed Roger a beer and opened his own.

"Columbus Day coming up. Or should I call it Indigenous Peoples' Day," snorted Sam. He pulled on his beer a drank a long swig. "Don't you get the idea, Roger, that tens of millions of our fellow Americans are half crazy."

"More than half crazy. How about full crazy. That is the country we live in."

"Why do you think it got so crazy?"

"Sam, there's lots of reasons. Affluence. People got it so easy. But mostly it's the media, mostly it's television, and Hollywood. The television networks and Hollywood hate the old America. In their minds, the old America was evil and failed to live up to their liberal standards. George Washington. Thomas Jefferson. Andrew Jackson. Robert E. Lee. Teddy Roosevelt. They are to be cordoned off to a dark, dusty corner and be ignored, at best, or to be vilified, at worst."

"They hate our country."

"They hate our heritage, Sam. They hate our history. They hate our heroes. Hell, they hate us. You. Me. Probably they hate most of us country folks."

"I remember what Obama and Clinton said about us country folk. Obama said we clung to our guns and religion and our country ways. At least Hillary Clinton was honest enough to call us deplorables."

"That we are, in the eyes of many."

Sam chuckled and said, "You know, most of us country folks just want to live our lifestyle and not bother the city folks. We just want to be left alone. I just want to run my farm. I want to own my guns and shoot them off whenever I damned well please. I want to hunt. I want to fish."

"Yeah, Sam. Many of the folks in power want to micromanage other people's lives. Political power can be a drug to a certain sort of political person. History is filled with them. Communist Russia. Nazi Germany. The France of Robespierre and Napoleon. There is a sort of person with political power who despises anyone who doesn't live like them and wants to impose their values on the people they despise."

A flight of Canadian geese flew overhead, honking, and both men watched the geese. They descended into a small pond at the far end of the Wessinger property.

"Do you think that, deep down, they despise themselves?" asked Sam.

"No. They love themselves very much. They are all wonderful. No. But they hate what was before them. The past doesn't live up to their modern standards."

"I would hate to feel that way. Our ancestors weren't perfect. But they are our people. How can you turn your back on your own kin?"

Roger tapped the table. "I wouldn't. You wouldn't. But a lot of people turn their backs on their own folks. Millions don't even care about what their own people did long ago. It's the past. You know, history is rarely pretty. A lot of the things were done in the past that are considered evil today. But these things that were done built a civilization out of a wilderness. The pioneers and the builders did a pretty good job. Imperfect, yes. But they did a pretty good job."

Becca stepped out of the house and cheerfully said, "And look who the wind brought in. Hello, Roger. How are you, sweetie?" Becca walked over to Roger and gave him a powerful hug. She was a large, roundish woman with dark brown hair that was graying at the roots. Becca was wearing a red cooking smock over a long dress of rust-and-gold flowers scattered over a white background. Apple stained part of her smock. She had a glass of white wine in her hands.

"It is always a pleasure to see you, Becca," said Roger. Becca had been best friends with Roger's younger sister, Anna Mae.

"What have you been doing with yourself?" asked Becca as she sat down in a chair to Roger's left.

"Getting the last of the apples in. I'm making the rounds today and finding out which stands need more apples. Once I finish with apple season, I'd like to take some time off."

"Can't say that I blame you. It's been a hard year for you," said Becca and she wiped at her left eye. It had teared. Becca Wessinger was a woman of great heart who loved her friends, laughed with them in good times, and cried with them in sad times.

"Are you thinking of traveling somewhere, Roger?" asked Sam.

"Yeah. I think I'd like to." Roger looked at Sam and then at Becca. "I think I'd like to visit the Maryland Eastern Shore where Connie was from. I haven't been there for years. Most of Connie's people are dead or have moved on or weren't close to begin with. Only an aunt showed for the funeral. Once Connie got the teaching job in Stonewall and then married me and we had children, she lost contact with most of her family. Her parents divorced when she was in college. Her mother moved to Vermont after the divorce and ran a bed-and-breakfast with her second husband. She came to the wedding, and we never saw her again. Connie's dad was a drunk with an inheritance. He moved to Key West and lived the Margarittaville life until he fell off his sailboat drunk one night. I guess he died happy."

Becca smiled. "I loved the crabcakes Connie made. And the crab soup. Dear Connie was quite a cook and a lot of fun," she said. "Yeah, she was a dear woman."

"How did she end up moving to Stonewall to teach?" Sam asked. "I always wondered about that."

"The state recruited teachers from out of state in those days. I don't know that they still do. Connie was an accredited teacher and moved west to work. Simple as that."

"And then she met you," Becca said, and she chuckled.

"Yeah, she did. I had just moved back to Stonewall after working a series of jobs in and about DC. I was glad to be out of DC and glad to be living among normal people. Most people in DC aren't normal. And then I met a school teacher named Connie."

"Yes, you did," said Becca.

"The best thing that ever happened to me," said Roger.

"You know it," said Sam.

His second beer done, Roger rose from the chair. "Got to go, friends. I have a few more places to visit on my rounds. Going by Annie's next."

"She's not been well lately," said Becca. "Got a sore hip. Probably arthritic. She might need a hip replacement."

"Annie told me of her woes the last time I was by her stand. She's a good old girl, that's the truth. Getting old ain't much fun. But she's got a lot of gravel in her," said Roger.

Sam and Becca stood, and Becca gave Roger a big hug, and Roger kissed her cheek. Sam shook Roger's hand and said, "See you later, Roger."

"See you, Sam." Roger stepped off the porch and onto the grass.

"Canning green beans next Saturday, Roger. Are you in?" asked Becca.

"Sure. Just give me a call," answered Roger. Roger and Connie often canned vegetables and fruit with the Wessingers in the past.

Roger strolled over to his truck and drove off. Two minutes gone from the Wessingers, and Roger reached the main road to Paw Paw. Annie's Farm Stand was fifty yards down the main road away from Paw Paw. He turned left into the gravel in front of Annie's stand and came to a stop. But Annie wasn't there.

Annie's Farm Stand was open air with a roof, fifteen feet long with rows of shelving, and was painted white. Her vegetables had been sold out for weeks. Apples and her homemade preserves, jams, and jellies lined the shelves. Prices for the items were handwritten on white index cards. A large glass that looked like it had been part of a child's aquarium sat on one of the middle shelves. Written out on an index card that was taped to the glass were the words *Honor System* in black Magic Marker. Two inches of green paper sat at the bottom of the glass. Roger reached in his wallet, took out a five-dollar bill, dropped it into the glass, and grabbed a small jar of blackberry jam. It was a favorite.

Roger reached for another beer as he drove south on the road. He opened the beer with a paint-can opener he always kept in his truck. Then he poured the beer into his travel cup, careful to slant the cup so the beer wouldn't foam too much and overflood the cup. It was his fourth beer of the day, and he felt good.

The highway sloped up and then down like a series of mountainous waves. To his right, Roger passed the Judson farm, a big farm with a white barn and a grain silo larger than the Wessingers'. Henry Judson was a county commissioner. A large sign the size of a car sat at the front of the property and said *Thank You Jesus* in bright yellow against a white background. Scores of cattle grazed about the big property. The Judson house was big and white with a wraparound porch with four large pillars. Roger passed the smaller Sloan ranch next. It had a couple dozen cattle. The Sloans had their own sign, and it read Jesus Saves in a bold red. Their house was smaller, built in the late 1800s, and was white. Two hundred yards past the Sloans but on the left-hand side of the highway was a small house with a sign that said *Donley's Deer Processing*. Fred Donley had butchered deer for years just as his father had. He worked the rest of the year as a handyman who wasn't often handy and was only a willing worker when he really needed the money. After deer season, Donley rarely worked outside of his house until the Spring.

After Roger passed a couple of beat-up and rusted trailers, he drove up to a hand-painted sign that read *Assembly of God Church* in red with *Apple Butter for Sale* written below with an arrow pointing left down the Coakley Mountain Road. Roger took the left and in a mile was at the church. At a small table in the church parking lot, Steve and Melissa Householder were selling apple butter. Roger stopped the truck and walked up to the Householders.

"Quite an operation you're running here, Mr. and Mrs. Householder," said Roger as he walked toward the couple. "How much is the apple butter?"

"Ten dollars, Roger. Fundraising for the church," replied Steve. Melissa Householder's apple butter was well-known in much of the county. It was always on sale this time of the year after the apple crop had been picked. The Householders had bought their apples from Roger, and it was only neighborly that Roger bought apple butter from them. Roger enjoyed eating the Householder apple butter on a muffin.

"Is ten enough?" quipped Roger.

"Our church takes donations," said Melissa. Melissa was a tall, big-boned woman who kept her hair in a gray-brown bun. She was wearing a long gray skirt with a yellow blouse.

"What are you up to, Roger?" asked Steve. Steve stepped around the table and shook Roger's hand with both his hands. Steve was a roly-poly man with a nearly bald head and wore silver-framed glasses. He was one of those sorts of men who were perpetually cheerful and positive. Roger liked Steve very much unless Steve began to recite obscure Bible passages.

"I was just taking a drive about the country," replied Roger.

"Is it still here?" asked Steve.

"Blount County is still here, Steve. Not sure about anything else. Don't care much that is outside the county. The county is a real place, and so is the state. But the nation..." The three people chuckled.

"With the end of the tax exempt for churches, we'll have to do more fundraising. Good thing is that the property tax is so low here. There are benefits to living in comparative poverty. Glad not to live in the cities and the suburbs and live their lives of high taxes, high traffic, and the crowds." Steve paused and smiled. "I love this place."

"So do I. We're blessed."

"Why do you think the national government has ended the tax-exempt status on the churches?" asked Melissa. She sat down on a fold-out lawn chair.

"Because most churches don't abide by the national government's religion of secular liberalism. The powers that be cannot stand people who have values different than their own. Certain churches believe in sacred, absolute values of the past. So what does the government do? It can't outlaw religion. There's the First Amendment. But they can attack religion by putting an axe to the old concept of tax-exempt status for the churches."

"So they attack the churches with tax policy. Pretty dirty stuff," said Steve. "A lot of churches can't afford not to have tax-exempt status. A lot of them will go under."

"The national government is just too happy about that. Churches are not only a nuisance to the government, they are a rival to the government's secular religion."

"They won't kill us," answered Melissa. "Our church is humble just as the Lord, and His disciples were humble. We can live poor as long as we are true."

"That's the right way to think about it," said Roger.

Melissa pointed to the weathered white clapboard building with black double doors and two simple front windows. The building wasn't small but wasn't big either. It might fit a hundred people in it and maybe not.

"Do you think they'll ever go after the churches beyond the tax exempt, Roger?" asked Steve.

"No. Not in any way that will close them. But they think Christianity is an anachronism that will fade away. The popular culture has no use for Christianity. And the popular culture tries to mold the young away from Christian thought and Christian teachings."

"That they do," said Melissa with a shake of her head.

"The Bible is truth, you know," said Steve.

"Of course it is. But it is hard to explain the truth to children who are growing up in a world of schools who teach politically correct gobbledygook and the television shows that are more politically correct than the schools," said Melissa.

"It is a rotten, anti-Christian world we live in," said Steve.

"It may become more anti-Christian. The culture, that is," said Roger. "But I think that we'll be allowed to worship in private. Not in public so much. But the churches will remain open. And the powers that run the country don't really care about what happens up in the mountains. We don't count."

"Do you think we're in the end time, Roger?" asked Melissa.

"No. We should be. But we're not yet. Man survived Sodom and Gomorrah. It survived ancient Greece and ancient Rome and the French Revolution. It even survived the communists and the Nazis. God is tolerant of sin. I don't know why."

A half-dozen does darted across the road and into thick woods that extended from the church parking lot. Roger and the Householders watched the deer until they could not be seen or heard. The deer were deep into the woods in a flash.

"God's mercy is boundless," said Steve. His wife nodded.

"Yet most of us do very little to deserve God's mercy," said Roger. "I'm as guilty as anyone in taking God for granted."

"Even the most devout Christian takes the Lord for granted," said Melissa. "Why do you suppose?"

"Wealth," answered Roger. "We are so wealthy today. So many things to buy. Cars, trucks, washing machines, dishwashers, hot tubs, pools, antibiotics, open-heart surgery, the flush toilet. Can you imagine that most people who have ever lived never got to use the gadgets we take for granted? George Washington never used a flush toilet. Nor did Cleopatra or Julius Caesar or Napoleon. Martha Washington never used a dishwasher. Of course, she had a slave to wash dishes."

"And then man chose to believe science was the absolute truth," Roger continued. "Darwin told us that man evolved from apes. Man was not a divine creation. The Bible was fiction. God was not only dead, He never existed. The Big Bang created the universe and created the fish and the mammals and the trees and the oceans and the mountains and the human beings. Man could do anything. Religion was a drug, as Karl Marx maintained. Despite all the power mankind claims for itself, mankind is so unhappy. Man has so many material goods that man turns his back on the spiritual. Man desperately needs God's love."

A car with Washington, DC, tags pulled up to the stand. A slight man of about sixty wearing purple shorts and a gold-striped shirt on a black background stepped out of a Mercedes convertible. His gray hair was cut short. A younger man, very muscular and wearing tousled-up blond hair, remained in the car. He wore earrings on both ears and a spike through his nose.

The older man walked toward Roger and the Householders. He stopped ten feet away and asked, "Do you know where the resort is?"

"Which resort?" asked Steve.

"The Hadrian Resort," the man replied.

"Never heard of it." Steve looked at Melissa and Roger. "Either of you heard of the Hadrian Resort?"

"I've never heard of it," replied Roger. Melissa didn't speak, but her expression was one of puzzlement.

"I don't know of any resorts in the county. What kind of resort are you talking about?" asked Steve.

The man grinned. "It is a clothing-optional resort."

"Clothing optional. What do you mean by that?" asked Melissa. Her face had a shocked look on it now.

Amused, the man answered, "Where all the people can walk about naked. Not a stitch of clothes on. Free and easy. To live in nature naked is really a healthy way to live."

"Women go about naked too?" asked Melissa.

"Sure. Totally naked."

"Aren't they embarrassed being naked in front of men they don't know? Men not their husbands?"

"No. It suits them fine. Not that I care to see a woman naked," said the man. He looked over at his car and the man inside. He chuckled. "Naked women don't interest me at all. I'm not a breeder."

"A breeder? What do you mean?" asked Melissa.

"A man and a woman breed. I'm not into that. I'm into a different sort of love."

"What?" Melissa face had turned red.

"You see that young stud in my convertible? My Justin is twenty-four and ripped. He bench-presses four hundred pounds. He's the love of my life. Or at least until I get bored with him. I could get bored with him this weekend, and I'll have to find another love of my life. But I think Justin will last the weekend. Unless I find a stud more interesting at the resort. You never know. Being gay means not being tied down to some obsolete convention and the ridiculous institution of marriage. So old-fashioned."

"None of us know of the resort you are talking about," said Steve. "Sorry."

"What are you selling?" asked the man.

"Apple butter," replied Steve. "We're fundraising for our church."

"Your church. Sorry. I don't think so," said the man. He shook his head. "Churches are so intolerant. I have no use for them. Sorry to offend but not really." He turned and walked back to his car. In a moment, he was gone with the younger man.

"I do declare," said Melissa after the car was safely away.

Steve shook his head. "I wouldn't think our mountains would have such a resort."

Roger grinned. "Infiltration, I suppose. Actually, it makes a lot of sense. The mountains are beautiful. A gift from God. But the land is cheap, and the capital is only a few hours away. And there are some sellers up here. Not many. But they do exist." Roger picked up a jar of apple butter from the table and handed Melissa a ten-dollar bill. "Thanks for the apple butter, Mr. and Mrs. Householder. Got to get going."

"God bless you, Roger," said Melissa.

Roger drove down Coakley Mountain Road and was quickly in a heavily wooded expanse. The road inclined slightly but remained about as straight as a road in the mountains could be. He passed one rough-cut road to his left. It was a logging trail that served the forests owned by the Maley family. Fifteen seconds later, Roger came up to an 18-wheeler loaded with log poles coming the opposite way, and he edged his truck to the right to give the logging truck more room. The truck thundered by with the bounty of the forest. Roger opened another beer, poured it into the travel cup, and drank a sip.

The road cut sharply to the right and then banked left. Roger passed an old mobile home with two cars sitting on a small gravel driveway. One of the cars sat on cinder blocks. Two scruffily dressed middle-aged men smoking cigarettes looked over the car on the blocks. It was an old Buick LeSabre from the nineties.

The road went down now, curling one way for a short distance and then curling back in the opposite direction for a short distance. In a small clearing, Roger passed an ugly mass of rusted junk inside a short wood fence missing half its slats. Four ravaged mobile homes. Several washing machines. Two tractors. Five or six refrigerators. A couple of dryers. A stove with its burners ripped out. A riding lawn mower. Three cars that looked at least fifty years old. Crates. A gas pump that read *Texaco Fire Chief*. Two motorcycles. A sofa and a recliner. A Coca-Cola machine from the sixties. A Bayliner fishing boat with a split hull. A basketball backboard. It was a stain on the land. Roger didn't know who owned the forsaken, abandoned land. Who paid the property taxes? Or did the county government even care to collect taxes on the land?

Roger continued driving down toward the river, leaving the trash heap behind. The road ended abruptly at the Black Elk River Road. The Black Elk River Road ran along the river, winding along the contours of the Black Elk but above the stream, often very high above the river. Sometimes the road was a close as ten feet above the river, but sometimes it was as high as one hundred feet above the river. Portions of the road stood on sheer cliffs above the river with steep ravines that hedgehogged down to the river. Driving off the road meant catastrophe as old forests of sturdy trees dominated the ravines. Many of the trees were from the days long ago when the mountains were virgin and wild. But wasn't much of the mountains still wild? Weren't the people of the mountains part wild, a reflection of their environment? Roger mused how the mountains and its rivers molded the people who lived and died in the mountains. The mountains were in the blood of the people.

The road was thin and sparingly accommodated two cars. Yellow reflectors had been installed at a few areas where the road was thinnest and the ravines were highest and most dangerous. Some parts of the road saw erosion of the pavement, and a road crew would eventually have to restore the road and make it safe again.

Roger came up to a modern house close to the river. It was a gray Cape Cod and very handsome, with a wraparound porch and two-car garage. A Washington lawyer named Braden Debevois owned it as a weekend home. He and his wife were rarely there in the winter but came fairly often the rest of the year. They were unpopular with their neighbors. Anita Debevois made it a habit to yell at hunters in adjoining fields and try to frighten away deer. One day, soon after the house was built, she went as far as yelling at Charlie Benkonback and slamming two pots together when he was hunting in woods he leased adjacent to the Debevois property. Benkonback did not take the intrusion very well and fired his Mossberg up in the air, frightening the woman. Braden Debevois called the Sheriff's Department, and Sheriff Bixler unsuccessfully explained how unneighborly it was in Blount County to interfere with a hunter. At first, Benkonback refused to apologize, but Sheriff Bixler explained that the situation called for it. Debevois was wealthy and was a lawyer and had a snitty wife and could throw his weight around. Benkonback made an apology he never meant, and the situation was resolved although the situation was never really resolvable. Nobody hunted in land near the Debevoises' property since then, and Braden and Anita Debevois became pariahs in the county. They didn't belong in the mountains.

The Black Elk was an anarchic river full of turns and twists. It was also very shallow. Rocks abounded, large and small. At many points, a man could cross it by stepping on rocks and not get very wet. Downed trees lined the shore. The deep woods that surrounded the river were reluctant to allow sunlight to the river below, and many parts of the river were half dark most of the time. For a wild river, the Black Elk was peaceful most of the time. The rapids were many but not especially turbulent. The Black Elk rarely overflowed its banks, and this usually happened after a large snowmelt or a very heavy and sustained rain. When the river swelled with water, the current could be strong and violent. All but the biggest rocks would be covered, and a man could no longer cross the river and stay dry.

The road wound for two miles without a house or a grazing animal. Roger began a slow descent and began to edge away from the Black Elk River. This remote section of the road ended suddenly as Roger approached the two-hundred-acre Whitacre farm. Twenty cattle fed and drank near a small pond on the Whitacre farm. The Whitacre farm was flatland placed in a small valley. The Whitacre house sat far back from the road. It was a handsome farmhouse and was painted white with blue shutters on the many windows. Two porches, one above the other, ran down the front of the house. The barn nearby was ramshackle and not painted for the most part, except for a faded Mail Pouch chewing-tobacco advertisement painted on the side that faced the road. The Whitacres were one of the most ancient families in the county and dated from the eighteenth century. Tad Whitacre owned this farm, but he had at least a half-dozen Whitacre relatives who also farmed nearby.

The Whitacre farm gone from view, the Black Elk River Road banked right for a quarter mile and came a little closer to the river. Then the road jutted to the left, and Roger came upon the simple clapboard house of the Stillwells. A flagpole with a sole Confederate flag dominated the small front yard of the Stillwells. Ben Stillwell, fat and red-faced and dressed in blue jeans and a blue flannel shirt, sat in an old house chair on the front porch smoking a cigarette and drinking a can of beer. This branch of the Stillwell family had lost most of its land three or four generations before. These Stillwells worked as members of road crews, drove school buses, operated excavating equipment, pumped out septic tanks, repaired cars and tractors, and clerked convenience stores. Ben was sixty and didn't work. Roger believed Ben was on disability but wasn't sure. It wasn't Roger's business to know, and he and Ben weren't friends. Almost all the Stillwells in the county—and there must have been a hundred of them—took advantage of the SNAP program and the food giveaways that most churches in the county put on. When a family lost most of its land in the mountains, the family fell far.

Right ahead of Roger was a large red streak on the road, and a four-point buck lay dead at the end of the streak near a gulley. That was expected in the early fall. Deer became more active and bolder.

And more would be killed by cars. Hunting season was next month, and more deer would be killed. Those deer hunted in November would be butchered for food. But roadkill deer would rot or be eaten by the vultures or the foxes.

Black Elk River Road ended at the town of Four Churches. Four Churches was named in the long past. It was but a small hamlet now and only a rundown Baptist Church remained. Roger turned onto the main road back to Stonewall. He drank a sip of beer. There's nothing like cold beer to keep you company on a drive through the mountains. Ralph Buckner's stand was a half mile up the road to Stonewall, and Roger could see that Ralph was getting ready to close. Roger pulled into the gravel-and-dirt driveway, bringing up dust as he braked his truck.

"Hey, Roger," Ralph called out as Roger stepped out of the truck.

"Buck, how are you? Busy?" asked Roger.

"Not really. I don't know if I had ten customers today. A sweet day to be outside once the morning rain went away. But no business."

Roger walked over to Ralph and slapped the older man lightly on his left shoulder. Ralph Buckner was of medium build, and his hair was mostly white. He kept a billy-goat beard of white, and his eyes were sky blue. A reddish scar ran down the right side of his lower face just below the ear to his lower cheek and then to his chin. Ralph got the wound in an accident when he served in the army as a young man.

"Ready for fall?" asked Roger.

"Ready or not, fall is coming."

"That's right."

"I love the fall."

"It's a fine time of the year. I like the crispness of the weather and the drop in the humidity. A little cool and a little warm."

"I'm an old man, and I still love the changing of the colors on the leaves. That'll be right soon. The green leaves will change to gold and burnt orange and bright yellow and red. I especially love the red leaves. I still feel wonder at the change of colors in the leaves in the fall. But I feel mournful too. The change of colors means I have another year in the books," said Ralph and he chuckled. "The journey of life is closer to the end than the beginning. At least for me."

"Yeah, I'm closer to the end than the beginning too. You know, Buck, fall is beautiful but fall is the beginning of the end of life. Most of the trees lose their leaves, the fruit on the trees die, the vegetables left in the fields die. The world seems to lose its vibrancy. Maybe fall is so beautiful because so much life dies in winter."

"Fall is beautiful in itself. The change of the colors of the leaves. The change of the activities of the deer. The change of temperature. All that sort of thing."

"In the mountains," said Roger, "we live in a sort of rhythm of life. The summer brings life, and we enjoy the bounty. The food we grow ourselves in our land. Tomatoes. Corn. Green beans. Peppers. Lettuce. I wouldn't want to live any other way."

"I wouldn't want to live another way either. I like how we live independently here in the mountains."

"But are we so independent, Buck? Half the county gets food assistance from the government."

"But they're just playing the system. Just like the big fellas in Washington. The arms dealers. The drug dealers. The government workers. Unions. Big business. All the big shots who pay government men to do their bidding. The system is corrupt."

"The system is vile."

There was a silence between the two men that lasted a moment. Then Ralph chopped his right hand into his left and chuckled. "Roger, I could use a few bushels of apples to finish out the season."

"How many?"

"Five should do. But not right yet. Drop by in a week or so. And whatever I don't sell, Carol and I'll make apple butter out of."

"Sounds like a good idea. I'll be back in a few days with your apples. Friday about all right?"

"Sure. Friday's fine." The two men shook hands, and Roger was off again.

Roger opened up another beer for the ride back to Stonewall. He wasn't sure whether he was on his sixth or seventh beer. No matter. He felt fine. The ride back to Stonewall went well. He passed farms of families long part of the mountains: the Hardestys, the Krusbergs, the Daltons, the Mintons, the Dales, the Oates. Two centuries of work and blood and good times and births and deaths. The national government couldn't take that away.

There were businesses along the road back to Stonewall. Chip Dillon's auto repair shop in a white cinderblock building. Mel Dobson's small engine repair. He was the man to see for fixing chainsaws, lawn mowers, log splitters, and grass trimmers. Visits to Mel's took at least fifteen minutes because of the old man's ability to tell stories. The younger Baldwin boy, Neil, distilled whiskey in an unpainted shack that had been a small barn. His sign was hand-painted. Clarence Bishop sold antiques from an old service station long closed.

His traveling complete, Roger entered Stonewall from the west. It was getting late, and he hadn't thought of supper. So he pulled back into Mike's Diner.

Beth Grayson was the waitress for supper. Beth had protruding buttocks that looked absurd in her tight blue jeans. Her blouse was simple and black. Her hair was curly and dirty blond, and she kept it cut at the shoulders. Her face was moon shaped and jolly. On both of her meaty arms were garish red tattoos, one of a star and the other of a horse. Beth was in her early fifties and had waitressed at Mike's for as long as he could remember. Like many of the working women of Blount County, Beth was not married but was a mother.

Mike's was not crowded when Roger entered the restaurant. Mike's was rarely as busy for supper as it was for breakfast. Roger walked over to a corner table and sat down. Beth looked over from the counter and saw Roger. Beth picked up a laminated menu and her order book, and she walked over to where Roger had sat down.

"Hi, Roger. How are you?"

"Doing fine, Beth."

Beth placed the menu in front of Roger. "What are you drinking?"

"I've had enough beer for today. How about a sweet iced tea?"

"One iced tea coming up," said Beth and she walked back to the kitchen.

Only two other tables were taken at Mike's. A middle-aged couple that Roger did not know sat at a table at one end of the restaurant near a window. They were eating their meals and talking little. Clyde and Betty Stovall sat at the opposite end of the restaurant near a window. They had yet to be served. Clyde owned the Laundromat in town. Food was cooking in the kitchen, and Roger could smell steak sizzling on the grill.

Beth returned to Roger's table with the iced tea. "What'll you have, Roger?"

"A slab of meat loaf, mashed potatoes, and green beans." Roger handed the menu to Beth.

"Ketchup with the meat loaf?"

"No. I don't eat meat loaf with ketchup."

"That's right. I remember. You never eat meat loaf with ketchup." Beth marked her order book.

"I don't use ketchup for much. On a hamburger and that's about it."

"Neither do I. But my granddaughter is partial to it. Likes it on hot dogs, even."

Roger grinned. "Is that so? How old is Kayla now and what grade is she in at school?"

"My pride and joy is eight. Nine in February. Kayla's in the third grade."

"Does she like it?"

"She likes some classes and hates others. Just like all school kids."

"What does she like the most?"

"She likes to read, Roger. I don't think Kayla cares much about grammar, but she likes to read. Reading all the time." Beth stood with her right hand on her ample right hip. It wasn't busy, so she had time on her hands.

"Bet she hates history."

"How could you guess?" Beth smiled.

"Most kids don't like history. Especially girls."

"Ain't that the truth. And today they teach the children to hate themselves. Hate their heritage. Hate their ancestors." She shook her head.

"I bet. George Washington isn't the father of his country anymore. He's the evil slaveowner." Roger continued. "Hey, how's Danielle?"

"Living with her new boyfriend. Down south in Rexford. She works in a bank as a cashier."

"Do you like the young man?"

"Just met him once. I don't really know him. Nice enough. He works as an exterminator."

"It's work."

"Yep, it's work."

"Sometimes I wish Danielle lived in a way she could raise Kayla proper. But she's never had a stable relationship with a young man. So I'm the one raising Kayla like she's my own child. What's the world coming to? Grandmas raising children instead of their daughters. That's not natural. But I have to raise Kayla because it's my duty. And I love her so."

The cook called out from the kitchen, and Beth left Roger. She moved fast for a woman so fat. Twenty seconds later, Beth came out with food for the Stovalls and served them. Beth left the Stovalls, walked over, and checked on the other couple. She refilled drinks for the Stovalls and the other couple. Then the cook called out again, and Beth scrambled back to the kitchen. In a flash, Beth was walking back to Roger's table with a plate of meat loaf.

"There, Roger. Enjoy. Just let me know if you need a refill of tea. All right, sweetie?"

"You're too kind, Beth."

The food was simple and good. The meat loaf had a tomato sauce with a hint of liquid smoke. It didn't take Roger long to finish the food. He had skipped lunch. He was three-quarters done with his food when Beth walked over to him with a pitcher of iced tea and topped his glass.

"What do you do with yourself?" asked Beth.

"Apple season is winding down. The chickens are easy to keep. Same with the turkeys. The sheep are easy to keep. I drove about some today. Said hello to some people. Talked with the Wessingers for a while."

"How are they?"

"Fine. Becca was canning apple filling."

"Good for her. How's Grif?"

"Out of rehab. Didn't see him, though."

"Glad he's out. I hope it works out for him. The mountains have too many young people into drugs."

"Yeah, that's a fact. A damned shame too." Roger strummed his right hand against the table. "I saw the Householders at their church."

"Selling apple butter?"

"Right. They were selling apple butter. I bought some."

"You're sweet."

"Not really. I really like apple butter. I don't always breakfast here at Mike's. Most mornings I eat an English muffin with preserves or apple butter or sometimes peanut butter. And I might as well buy apple butter from friends. And the Householders are friends.

"Family and friends are what's important in life."

"True, Beth. So true." Roger smiled. "I'm thinking about taking a trip after all my apples are picked. Thinking about getting in my truck, filling it with gas and a little beer, and visiting where Connie was from."

"Where's that? I never knew where Connie came from, just that she wasn't from around here."

"The Eastern Shore of Maryland in crab country."

"I do declare. I never knew that she was from that far away."

"Oh yes. Connie picked crabs before she entered the first grade. At least that was her story."

"Is that right?" Beth chuckled and rolled her eyes. "I'm fifty-two, and I've never had a crab. Not one. Can you believe it?"

"Sure. There's no crabs in the mountains, that's for sure. People eat what's available where they live. I never ate a crab until I met Connie. The first time I ate a crab was when we visited childhood friends of hers on the Eastern Shore, and I ate crab lungs. I didn't know any better. There's nothing that tastes as bad as a crab lung. But I learned quick not to eat them again."

"When have you last been to the Eastern Shore?"

"Connie and I went about fifteen years ago. So it's been a long time. When it comes to crab, it's best to go to the source. In out of the way places on the Eastern Shore they have these shacks that process the crab. And there's still watermen in their white wooden boats crabbing the Chesapeake. Nobody gets rich, that's for sure."

"I hope you have a fine trip, Roger Lee. And tell me about it when you get back."

"Gladly."

Roger finished his food, paid his bill at the counter, and left a generous tip on his table. He finished his iced tea and left Mike's to go home.

Roger was fishing the river three days later. He woke early, fixed a pot of coffee, cooked an English muffin in the toaster, smeared the Householders' apple butter on the muffin, and had a quick breakfast. The morning air was brisk but not too cold, a fine fall morning. The sun was only beginning to rise above the mountain that encased the river on its east side. A flock of Canadian Geese flew overhead as Roger opened his back door. That was the first Canadian geese he had seen since they left in March.

Roger sat on a chair on his outdoor back porch and forced on his black rubber wading boots. Boots on, he began walking with his fly rod in his left hand and a bottle of beer in his right. He could hear the gentle rush of the river over the rocks a quarter mile away. The hummocky land nearest the house sloped in a gradual, easy decline to the river. Roger passed scrub pines that were scattered about the land. A copse of black walnut trees halfway down provided attraction for deer, but there were no deer this morning. Roger hadn't expected any.

He reached the river in five minutes. Trees lined the whole west bank of the river. With the mountain on one side of the river and the old-growth trees on the other side, little of the sun penetrated onto the river. The river was still very dark by the time Roger reached it. He sat down on a grassy bank and made sure the fly rod was fit for fishing. It was.

Roger walked over to a very rocky place near the river's edge and placed the bottle of beer in a small drop where the current was slow.

Only the top of the bottle stuck out of the water. Roger walked back to the bank, picked up his rod, and walked down the river where the fishing was best.

The Black Elk elbowed where Roger liked to fish best. The elbow caused a deepening of the stream that was three or four feet deep. There were few rocks to snag the line here. The fish preferred the relative shelter of the elbow rather than being forced into the rapids or the shallows of the river.

Roger cast the rod a dozen times before a fish hit. The fish hit fairly hard and struggled gamely, but Roger could tell it was small. He reeled in a sunfish that was smaller than the size of Roger's hand. He unhooked the fish, held it in the river for ten seconds, and released the fish.

He hooked a much-larger fish a minute later. It fought mightily and took out some line. It must be a smallmouth. He slowly reeled the fish in. It fought on. Roger slipped on a rock and stumbled forward and was on one knee for a second. He raised, still reeling in the bass. The fish was desperate and full of fight. Roger reeled in some more. And then the bass was out of the water and into Roger's hands.

Roger did not like to eat bass. He considered the bass a fun fish to catch for sport but not one he would eat. Roger held the bass in the river and freed it, and it darted away.

Three more bass were caught in half an hour. Roger released all three as he did the first bass. It was a lot of fun fishing the river, and Roger was glad he lived in such a place. Happy, Roger walked over to where he had put the beer. My, it was cold. Almost icy. He reached into his wet blue jeans and pulled out a bottle opener and opened the beer. It was a delicious beer, the first of the day. Roger reflected that the first beer of the day was the best beer of the day. All beer was good except for light beer, but the first beer of the day was special.

Saturday, Roger was back on the Wessinger farm to can green beans with the Wessingers and their close friends, the Baileys. A large picnic table and two folding tables sat on a concrete slab under an overhang that jutted out from the rear of the Wessinger home. To the right of the tables was a double burner with a large canning pot and a single burner with a small cooking pot. Four chairs sat at each side of the picnic table.

Sue Ann Bailey was tall and chunky and had a sunny disposition. She kept her dark brown hair medium short and a little unkempt. The waves of her hair were brushed away from her forehead, but small flashes of hair were swept forward across her forehead. Phil Bailey was called Bear by his friends because of his large size. Bear was tall, and his body was that of a football tackle who no longer exercised. Bear Bailey had a large head, and he kept a scruffy full beard that had white streaks in it. His uncombed and thick hair matched the beard, except for a bald spot at the center of his head that was the size of a softball. His hands were meaty and large.

On the picnic table sat four white rectangular plastic cutting boards and several sharp knives. On the smaller of the two folding tables sat a fifty-pound mesh bag of green beans Sam had bought for ten dollars from an Amish family that lived in the north part of the county. On the other table sat six-dozen quart jars still wrapped in boxes with plastic.

Sue Ann sat at the picnic table in front of one of the cutting boards with a wine glass half full of white wine. Bear and Sam Wessinger were standing away from the tables and near the double-burner drinking bottles of beer. Roger walked over from his truck to Bear and Sam.

"What are you people up to?" asked Roger as he approached.

"What do you think?" replied Bear with a loud laugh, and he slapped Roger on the shoulder. "Just drinking beers and taking it easy." Bear stuck out his right hand and Roger shook it. His right hand disappeared in Bear's paw. Bear pulled Roger toward him and gave him a manly hug. "Great to have you here," said Bear.

"I thought this was going to be a working party?" asked Roger.

"Sure is," said Sam.

"Just waiting for you, Roger," said Bear.

"Yeah, we're going to be working a bit this afternoon," said Sue Ann.

"Got that right," said Sam.

"I'll be ready," said Roger, "once I get my breath back. I've just been crushed by a bear. Hey, where's the beer hiding?"

"I've got a cooler right over there," replied Bear, pointing to a big white cooler near the back door of the house. "That miserable red cooler beside it is Sam's, and it's full of cans of Busch. My cooler has the good beer."

"Don't be messing with my Busch," said Sam with a laugh.

Becca came out the back door as Roger walked over to Sue Ann. "Glad to see you could make it, Roger," said Becca. She wore a long blue denim dress. She had a small round container of peanuts in her left hand, and she placed the peanuts on the picnic table next to a bag of pretzels. Roger gave Sue Ann a hug and a kiss on her right cheek.

"Who's doing the cutting?" asked Roger as he went over to the cooler and grabbed a beer. We walked back to the table, circled it to where Becca sat next to Sue Ann, and gave Becca a hug and a kiss.

"You, for one," said Becca. She stood and went back inside the house.

"All right. But why do I always get stuck with cutting in these get-togethers?" Roger sat down at the picnic table on the other side of Sue Ann.

"It's not that you're especially good at cutting," Bear called out. He laughed heartily. "It's because I'm so clumsy with a knife that doesn't have steak on it."

Roger shot back, "You're lazy. You just want to watch the jars of beans seal in the canner. And you want your hands free to get to the beer cooler. I know you."

"Hey, making sure the beans are sealed right is the most important job in this sort of operation. Anybody can cut and stuff the beans in a glass jar. But sealing the jars is complex and difficult and must be done with great care," said Bear.

"Great care my ass," said Sam.

"You mostly don't want to cut because those big hands aren't nimble enough to get the work done right," said Sue Ann. "You and a sharp knife aren't meant for each other. Unless you're gutting a deer."

Sam called out, "If Bear cut enough green beans, he'd surely lose a finger."

"That's right," said Sue Ann. She smiled and drank some wine.

Becca walked back outside with a glass of white wine in her right hand. She sat down at the picnic table and said, "Let's get cutting. That's what we're here for." She looked over at her husband. "Sam. Come and cut with us, sweetheart."

Sam dutifully walked over to the picnic table, picked up the fifty pounds of green beans as he passed the folding table, and put it down at the center of the picnic table. He sat down and placed his beer by his side. Becca grabbed a large handful of green beans, and Sue Ann, Roger, and Sam did the same. They began cutting.

Becca said, "Remember to cut the tips off. Both ends." She pointed to a small white plastic bucket near the green beans. "When you get enough tips, put them in the white bucket. We'll feed them to the chickens later on." Becca pointed to a large blue bucket on the other side of the green beans. "Put the beans that we're going to can in the blue bucket. Use your own judgment on whether you cut a bean in half. Think about how you like to eat a green bean.

"Six inches is too big, right?" asked Sam with a smile on his face. He held up a long green bean that he had tipped.

"It certainly is," said Sue Ann. "Chop that in half, Sam."

"I'd say six inches is a bit on the small side," said Bear as he was attaching the propane tanks to the burners.

"You would say that," said Sue Ann. "But you have an exaggerated sense of size. Always have."

"So six inches is as big as it gets," said Roger.

"Sure is, sweetie," said Becca. "Anything larger, cut it in half. We don't need a bunch of long beans."

The four of them were knifing the green beans, cutting the tips to the side in little piles. The blue bucket was being filled with segments of green beans. Bear was fidgeting with the propane tanks and drinking beer. He got the single burner going, and the water inside began to heat. It was Bear's job to fill the quart jars with green beans and add a tablespoon of salt and some of the boiling water. Then we would screw on the lids. Bear would place the quart jars of green beans aside on the little folding table until he had enough to start sealing them in the pressure canner.

"You're mighty fast, Sue Ann," said Roger.

"A lot of practice. Oldest girl in a big family. It's important to be fast with a knife."

"She's lightning fast with the knife, Roger," Bear called over. "Glad she's never come after me."

"There's always a first time," Sue Ann replied with a short laugh.

"Never a safe moment at the Bailey house," said Bear.

Becca was fast with the knife as well, maybe faster than Sue Ann. She cut the tips, brushed them aside to a pile, and cut the main stalk of the green bean into a larger pile. Every minute or so, she would cup the green beans and put them in the blue bucket. She was a machine, the fastest of the four.

"Tommy Barber is selling half his herd," said Sam. The Barbers had forty acres a mile away from the Wessingers. "Say's he's too old to handle so much cattle. And Jasper Barber is going to stay with the state police until he reaches pension age, so he ain't there to help very often."

"And Rennie Barber ain't worth a damn," said Bear. He shook his head.

"Drugs and liquor isn't a good combination," said Becca.

"Ain't that the truth," replied Bear.

"Isn't Tommy close to seventy?" asked Sam.

"Yes, he is," said Roger. "He was part of that team that went to the state semis way back."

"He was a tough man. Still is. Just got old and his body got beat," said Bear, and he downed the rest of his beer and went to the cooler. "Who's ready for another?"

"Get me another, will you?" answered Roger. "Almost finished this one."

"I'm fine," said Sam. He grabbed a handful of peanuts, put all of them in his mouth, and chased the peanuts with a large swallow of beer.

The cutting continued, and the water on the single burner began to boil. The pile of green beans in the blue bucket rose to over a foot high and then two. Becca used her bare hands to even out the pile in the bucket. Minutes after Becca smoothed the pile, Bear

41

began filling the quart Mason jars. He filled the jars to the top with green beans and added the salt and the boiling water. He placed the seal within the aluminum ring and screwed them tightly to the jar threads and then set them aside. Bear would begin pressure canning the beans once he had twenty-three quarts to fill the canner.

"Ready for winter, Roger?" Sam asked.

"It's coming whether I like it or not. Easily my least favorite season," Roger replied.

"The only thing good about winter is getting the wood stove cranked up and running," said Sue Ann.

"Florida would be a nice place to be in winter," said Bear as he screwed on a lid. "That's seventeen ready. I'll be canning soon."

"That's fine, Bear," said Becca. She stood. "Do you want a refill of wine, Sue Ann?" she asked.

"Sure," replied Sue Ann, and she handed her glass to Becca but Becca did not grab it.

"I may as well bring the rest of the bottle," said Becca, and she began walking toward the back door. She reached the back door, opened it, and turned her head and called out, "Anyone in the mood for whiskey?"

"Count me in," answered Bear.

"Sure," said Roger.

"I'm in too," said Sam.

Becca came back out with the rest of the bottle of wine in her left hand and a bottle of whiskey in her right. She placed the bottles on the table with the green bean quarts and then pulled three shot glasses out of the right pocket of an apron she had put on. She poured whiskey in each glass and gave each man a whiskey. Bear downed his in one gulp and smiled.

"Talked with Mac last week. Says the government has contacted him about long-gun registration," Roger said.

"I never turned in my handguns. I certainly ain't going to register my long guns. Ain't happening," answered Bear.

"That'll be impossible to enforce," said Sam. "Nobody up here in the mountains will ever comply with such a ridiculous government order. To hell with that."

"Local police will never go house to house looking for rifles and shotguns," said Sue Ann. She looked at Roger. "Why do you think the government would want to register long guns when they know nobody will do as they're told?"

Roger chuckled and said, "Of course, the government knows nobody will follow their orders. Mac isn't going house to house, and neither will the Sheriff's Department or the state police. But passing unenforceable laws does make us into criminals in the eyes of the national government. And that's what the national government wants. It gives them some sort of moral superiority. They are the legal force of virtue, and the people in the mountains are criminals."

"What kind of authority do they want?" asked Becca.

"A soft tyranny," replied Roger. "They don't want to micromanage us. That would cost too much time and money. And the whole world is bordering on bankruptcy."

"Hell, Roger, I kind of understand what you're saying," said Bear as he walked up to the bottle of whiskey. "But the national government can intimidate us, even me. I'm honest with my beliefs when I'm with my friends. But I watch out with people I don't know. Outsiders. Tourists." Bear poured himself a whiskey.

"It's like you can't say what you really believe when you go out to shop or eat," said Sue Ann. "Why did the country allow such a situation?"

Sam said, "The insanity moved slowly while people didn't realize it. Like a nasty old vine. And the culture changed so much since I was a boy. The country has become so vulgar."

"And it has affected us in the mountains too," said Becca. "Young women giving birth to babies out of wedlock is the normal thing to do just like they do in the city slum neighborhoods. And you can't just blame the stupid girls. The boyfriends—"

"Sperm donors," interrupted Bear.

Becca continue, "The boyfriends turn their backs on their own babies. No responsibility. The government and the grandparents are raising the babies and not the fathers."

"The whole thing is terrible," said Sue Ann.

Bear filled another jar with green beans, poured some of the boiling water inside the jar and a little salt, topped the jar with a lid, and screwed shut the jar. "That's twenty-three," he announced. He filled one of the canners with three inches of water, turned on the propane, and lit the burner with a six-inch lighter. Minutes later, the water began to boil. He placed a metal rack at the bottom of the canner and placed twelve jars on the rack with his big hands. He next placed another metal rack on the bottom row of jars and formed a top row of eleven jars. He shut the canner lid to the base of the canner and sealed it using the sturdy black plastic wing nuts.

"We should be on our way in a few minutes," said Bear.

"That's fine," said Becca. "We'll be finished cutting green beans in half an hour, I reckon."

"Can't come soon enough," said Sam as he halved a green bean.

"Just a little work, Sam," said Roger as he drank some beer. "Makes the beer go down sweeter by doing some work."

"Sweeter my ass," said Sam with a grin.

"Roger's right, you know," Sue Ann said. "You have to earn your beer, Sam."

"But it's my beer. I've already earned it," replied Sam. Sam looked over at Becca. "What do you have planned for real food?"

"Well, Sam, you might have noticed that Crock-Pot in the kitchen," replied Becca.

"No, I didn't," said Sam.

"Not surprised, sweetheart. I slow-cooked a pork shoulder for about eight hours yesterday and pulled it late last night after it cooled down. That's why I was up until ten. Sauced it this morning, and it's cooking on low right now. Made some coleslaw this morning too."

"Now that is an idea," said Bear.

"You bet," said Roger.

Steam came out of a small opening on the cover of the canner. Bear placed a ten-pound weight on the hole and then attached the pressure gauge onto another hole on the cover. Bear looked over at Becca. "Ten pounds weight for half an hour, right?"

"That's right, Bear," replied Becca.

The green beans finished pressure sealing a half hour later. Bear unfastened the wing nuts, and steam shot out of the canner. Bear placed the cover in the grass off the concrete slab. He next used plastic-coated tongs to pull out the jars and placed them on a folding table.

Ten minutes later, the cutting of the green beans was completed. Bear had already begun filling the jars, and the cutters began to help him out. Nineteen jars were filled with green beans, so Bear set a bottom row of ten and a top row of nine. He got the process going again, and a few minutes later the last of the green beans began to be pressure sealed. It was time to eat.

The five of them filed into the house. On the kitchen counter was the Crock-Pot of pork barbecue, a freshly opened pack of hamburger buns, a small stack of paper plates, and a large glass bowl filled with coleslaw. Each of the five reached for a plate, fixed themselves some food, and went back outside to eat at the large picnic table.

As Roger sat down at the picnic table, he saw that Bear was chomping down a mountain of barbecue topped with a layer of coleslaw, large bites of the sandwich getting devoured in the large jowls of the big man. Bear ate fast. Parts of his beard received green-and-white coleslaw bits.

"This is damned good," Bear announced. He drank a large swallow of beer.

"Slow down, Bear," said his wife, knowing that he would not abide.

"You like it, huh?" said Becca, looking over at Bear.

"It is mighty fine," said Sam. "Becca always does a great job with barbecue."

"That's for sure," Roger said after he finished his first bite. He kept the coleslaw separate from the sandwich.

"Ah, if you can't cook barbecue right, you might as well give up cooking," said Becca.

"All barbecue is good," said Bear. "But pork is my favorite. Chicken and beef are fine too, but not as good as pork. What do you think, Sam?"

"Pork is best. And for sauce, I like it more tomatoey than vine-gary. Some vinegar, yes. And some mustard too. But not too much," said Sam.

"I like it not too spicy hot. Some heat is fine. But not too much," said Sue Ann.

Becca said, "A lot of the greatness of barbecue is that it is best to cook it slow and not at too hot a temperature. Cook the meat a long time. That cooks the meat tender. Six, seven, eight hours is about best. Never rush the meat, for heaven's sakes."

Bear finished his first barbecue, wiped his mouth with his left hand, stood, and walked to get himself another.

"There's plenty," said Becca. "Eat as much as you want. That was a six-pound pork shoulder I crocked. Plenty of meat."

"I plan to eat my fill, Becca," Bear answered as he opened the back door and came outside. On his paper plate was another ham-burger bun filled with barbecue and coleslaw.

"Hey, does anyone want to do a shot with me?" asked Sam. He walked over to the folding table that had the bottle of whiskey.

"Sure, Sam," Roger replied.

"Me too," said Sue Ann.

"The more the merrier," said Roger. He drank from his bottle of beer. "Want a shot, Becca?"

"Why not?" she answered. "It's not like I'm driving anywhere tonight. That's your problem."

"Do you want a shot of whiskey, Bear?" asked Sam as he placed the bottle of whiskey on the picnic table. "Everybody else is."

"I'd be happy to," said Bear.

"Only three shot glasses. I'll go inside and bring out a couple more and get myself another barbecue," said Sam, and he went inside the house. He was back outside two minutes later, carrying a paper plate with a barbecue in his left hand and two shot glasses in his right.

"All right, time for a shot," said Bear. Sam handed the two clean shot glasses to Bear. Bear filled them and gave the two ladies each a shot of whiskey. Then he filled the men's shot glasses, spilling a little as he poured Roger's shot glass.

"Down the hatch," said Sam. All complied. Becca coughed after she drank her shot.

The friends continued to eat the barbecue. The three men drank beer, and the two women drank white wine. Becca opened a second bottle of white wine, a Chardonnay. The three men had another shot a half hour later and then another forty-five minutes after that.

Very late in the afternoon with the sun dropping fast, Bear asked Roger, "So do you have any plans this fall?"

"Yes. I'm going to the Eastern Shore of Maryland in a couple days."

"Why the Eastern Shore of Maryland?" Bear asked.

"I like it there, and I haven't been for quite a while. Connie was from the Eastern Shore."

"Does she still have family there?" asked Bear.

"I always wondered where Connie was from," interjected Sue Ann. "I knew she didn't grow up around here."

"Not much family anymore. Not anyone I'd want to look up. The family ties broke down. That's a sad thing to have had happen, but it happens all the time. Most families don't break apart, but they drift apart through indifference," said Roger.

"How long are you going?" asked Becca.

"A couple of days. My sheep should be fine inside the electric fence. The weather is still pretty fine. No rain on the horizon. I'll keep the chickens and turkeys in the coop," said Roger.

"When are you going?" asked Becca.

"Midweek, I think. Maybe Tuesday. Maybe Wednesday. Not having Connie around gives me more freedom. Not that I want it," said Roger.

"I know your heart must still be broken, Roger," said Becca, and the other three nodded.

"Yeah. That's the truth. You never know how much you miss someone dear when they're gone for good. It is so final," said Roger.

"She's with the Lord, Roger," said Becca. She reached over and patted Roger on the right shoulder.

"I'd like to think so," replied Roger.

"I agree. She was a sweet woman. Nobody better loved in Stonewall," said Sue Ann.

"Yep," Bear added, and he took another bite of barbecue. A morsel of pork fell into his beard, and he wiped his beard with his left hand. "She was a real sweetheart. Very dear. She had such a positive manner about her. You couldn't help but like her."

"A real lady," said Sue Ann. "She's missed. I miss her."

After a short pause, Sam asked, "Do you want Grif to come over to take care of your animals?"

"I would appreciate it. Maybe make sure the chickens and turkeys are watered and their feeder topped. I have three or four bags of feed in the barn. But I'll make sure to top their water and feed before I leave. And I'll make sure the sheep's water trough and feed trough are full," said Roger.

"I can slide on by too," said Bear. "That's what neighbors are for. That's what friends are for."

"In these crazy days in which we are living, it is our salvation to live deep in the mountains, woods, creeks, and rivers and away from the insanity in the cities and suburbs," said Roger with a chuckle.

"You can say that," said Bear.

Roger went on. "They think we're the uncivilized ones. We're uncultured people living in the sticks with our religious values, guns, conservative cultural values, canning parties..."

"You mean they don't have canning parties in New York, Chicago, Los Angeles, and Washington? I am surprised to hear that," said Sue Ann with a smile.

Becca laughed and said, "Dear child, those city folks probably think we're crazy canning our own beans in glass jars on a Saturday afternoon. Probably a lot of them would look at a jar and not know what to do with it other than to have a glass of iced tea in it. And they certainly wouldn't understand the friendship and good times of having a canning party."

"That's right," said Sam. "It's more than having green beans available that aren't soaked in salt water in a tin can. These green beans we canned today are real, not industrialized. Not part of the system. Independent of the system." Sam stopped a moment, looked over at the others, and chuckled. "I love this place."

Two days later, Roger was up at five thirty. He made a pot of coffee; watered and fed the chickens, turkeys, and sheep; and was soon driving out of Stonewall for his short trip. He figured it would take him four or five hours to get to the heart of crab country outside the ugly little city of Cambridge. He filled two plastic driving cups with black coffee for the trip and put six bottles of beer in a blue plastic cooler that had gashes in the plastic because of twenty-five years of use.

Roger floored the Ford truck to gain speed up the steep incline of Mount Bear Paw and was soon out of the little valley where Stonewall lay. He was beyond the town in a flash, speeding toward Virginia. The main road to Virginia wound about the mountains, up and down, angled right, and then left and back again like most roads in the mountains. It was still dark, and the beauty of the mountains didn't reveal themselves yet. There wasn't much to see except for the trees. Darkened houses. An occasional car going the opposite direction. In the rearview mirror, Roger could see headlights now and again, depending on the curves and rises of the road. A recently killed deer lay in a heap on the side of the road around a bend. Billboards advertising real estate and legal help were prominent along the road. The lawyers hawked legal help for divorce and workplace injuries at the top of their billboards. There was money to be made in misery.

Why do we need lawyers? Because we have laws. Lawyers specialize in making sense of laws. But do they make sense of laws? Because lawyers are specialists in laws, lawyers are experts in circumventing laws and altering laws. Good lawyers bend a law to fit the needs of their clients and themselves. So this made them vital to a society made of laws. Yet they really did no productive work. They did not build houses. They did not manufacture cars or trucks or washing machines or dishwashers or tractors or screwdrivers or shovels. Did any lawyer know how to use a tool beyond a hammer or a stapler? Lawyers did not care for the land and grow food for the people to eat. Lawyers were near the top of the pyramid, and what they produced was a confusing mishmash of laws that no sane person could keep track of. The lawmakers in Congress were a collection of lawyers who became wealthy but rarely did anything right.

Why aren't the productive people running things in Washington? Roger drank a sip of coffee as he drove out of the mountains and onto a flat valley. Maybe it had always been that way in the history of the nation. The Federalist Papers were written by two lawyers, James Madison and John Jay, and one who had his legal studies ended by the Revolutionary War, Alexander Hamilton. The Constitution was largely a creation of Madison and Hamilton. Sure, George Washington was not a lawyer but a soldier and farmer, a productive man. But most of the American presidents of the old days of national glory were lawyers. Thomas Jefferson. John and John Quincy Adams. Madison. Even Andrew Jackson, who had a difficult time spelling some of the simplest words in the English language, was a lawyer. He became president because of his success as a general, surely, but he wouldn't have become a general if he hadn't become a successful lawyer and politician first.

And even an Illinois railroad lawyer became a beloved president, idolized by millions. The candidate of Yankee business interests, Abe Lincoln, was also the man with the blood of 650,000 dead men on his hands. All Honest Abe had to do was allow the Deep South to leave the Union in peace and leave it to be a rural backwater with an anachronistic social system doomed to die when agriculture mechanized a few decades later. America would have still grown to be a continental power stretching from the Atlantic to the Pacific. America would have become a world power whether seven rural Southern states remained in the Union or not. But Lincoln had to conduct a war of conquest and destruction. His decisions killed 650,000 men. His decision in favor of war economically decimated a whole region of America. And yet he is on much of the national statuary and to condemn what he accomplished in the 1860s is to risk enmity and scorn. You could not say out loud what Roger Lee was then thinking if you knew what was good for you.

Polite society demanded that you turn your backs on and even condemn your ancestors, however heroic and manly they behaved in distant times. The men in gray who fought with empty bellies and without shoes were to be hated by their progeny because the elite hive thought it appropriate to shame the progeny into hating their own ancestors. So the statues of the famous were all torn down now. Lee. Jackson. Stuart. Davis. And so were the monuments that commemorated the sacrifices and valor of the average soldier. All torn down. The laws of Congress led to the tearing down of the statuary. A highway bill years ago had a rider attached that conditioned full funding of state highways on the removal of statues and monuments. So the legislators chose full funding of highways over the tributes to their dead kin. Unrooted, empty people. A wise man long forgotten called them hollow men without chests. Roger thought a moment. The great man's quote was on his lips. His memory wasn't all faded and gone. Yes. The great man wrote so long ago, "We make men without chests and expect from them virtue and enterprise. We laugh at honor and are shaped to find traitors in our midst." That was it. Roger was surprised he remembered it.

The mountains were fewer as Roger continued eastward away from the larger mountains. He was on Route 66 speeding about at eighty miles per hour in a world of 18-wheelers, trucks, and cars. Front Royal was in the rearview mirror now. He was speeding into the Virginia Hunt Country although the name was no longer true because foxhunts had been banned years before when Virginia was captured by the new elite that did not care for any of Virginia's history or traditions. It was still a little dark now, but light was filtering from the east. Roger knew of the Hunt Country and its land. The farms were wealthier than those of the mountains, but the ways of life were similar. People lived close to the land whether directly like a farmer or more indirectly when you worked a machine, or ran a store or worked for a bank filled with the deposits of the farmers. Roger's coffee was getting low, so he considered stopping for more, but then he decided against it. He had had enough coffee.

Closer to Haymarket, the sun was beginning to rise now, and Hunt Country petered out. Virginia was different here, no longer a land that the Washingtons, Jeffersons, Carters, Lees, and Byrds would recognize. What replaced the farms and green pastures and handsome country homes was an ugly mix of shopping centers with drab, block buildings; parking lots full of boring, utilitarian cars; planned developments where the houses all looked the same; and garish McMansions lined up close together, toe-to-toe, like offensive linemen at the goal line on fourth and a foot. How do people live like this, elbow to elbow, with so little privacy?

Construction workers in orange vests and plastic hats were cutting into the land with big machines, expanding Route 66. But was it to relieve current suburban traffic or was it to allow for the sprawl to desecrate more land to the west? There was more money to be made moving suburbia west into the Hunt Country and beyond. Would it reach the mountains? Probably the politicians and planners didn't know what the purpose of the expanded roads were for or that they had been duped by developer interests into thinking the building of more roads would alleviate the traffic problems that were never alleviated. The problem of traffic and sprawl in suburban Northern Virginia was self-perpetuating and never solved. Was an insolvable problem really a problem, a wise man from the midtwentieth century once asked? No, it was not a problem, he answered. It was a condition. Who wrote that? James Burnham, right? Yes.

Dump trucks brought in dirt and rock, and dump trucks were taking out dirt too, mostly red clay. Walls of concrete fifteen feet tall were being raised along the roads separating highway from houses. Backyards for some of the houses have been eaten away by steam shovels creating the new lanes of Route 66. The highway came first in this part of Virginia, and the families with backyards adjacent to the highways came second. Road before people. For the good of the suburban lifestyle. For the people in control of the government, the logic of the primacy of roads over people was sacrosanct. Anybody who thought elsewise was a Luddite.

Northern Virginia masqueraded as the American dream. But it was a world of nightmares. Four-thousand-square-foot homes that sold for a million dollars on tiny lots next to ten-lane highways undergoing constant construction. It was a world of congested roads and ubiquitous traffic jams, a world of angry motorists honking their car horns, drivers screaming at rude drivers more rude and vulgar than themselves, commuters disgusted with their commutes but unable to think outside the suburban mental box. These long, tedious commutes left these affluent suburban residents bone tired and mentally and emotionally broken by the time they reached their suburban paradises. And who were these children who spent most of their time on some computerized gadget instead of interacting with real people? Who could live this way? Only a neurotic person.

But several million did choose to live this way and couldn't think of living a different way. They lived under a regime of high property taxes. It was a world of affluent ugliness. Big homes on small lots with neighbors they barely knew or cared to know. On paper, those who live here should have been content and happy. Compared to the rest of the world or even the rest of the nation, they were the cream of the nation, wealthier than any upper middle-class in the history of the world. Instead, most felt an oppressive strain living in a wasteland of little joy. Northern Virginia was a purgatory of the hypercapitalist system that gave no love to the inhabitants but required the purchase of expensive homes, cars, gadgets, and government. Always more government.

Roger opened his first beer of the day, crossing the John R. Lewis Bridge spanning the Potomac River. It had once been named after Woodrow Wilson, but Wilson was no longer favored by the current regime running the government. Wilson was not a lawyer, mused Roger. He was worse. Wilson was a political scientist. That old sage from Baltimore had politicians pegged. Promises by politicians were almost never kept, and when they were, one group was looted to give plunder to a favored group. Modern government specialized in theft operating under the facade of democracy and elections. But modern democracy had more similarities to a cabal of medieval barons shaking down the peasantry than it did to the mystical version taught to brainwash callow schoolchildren. Roger did not mind that Wilson had been cast out into the outer darkness as Roger considered Wilson one of the worst figures of the American past. But the concept of obliterating the past bothered Roger. Abolishing the past did not start with Wilson and would not end with Wilson. It would be a continuing process.

It began to rain as Roger entered Prince George's County, and it was a very different world from Virginia. From his truck, Roger could see that the apartments and houses and shopping centers and strip malls had a beat-up, old look to them. Many of the shopping centers looked sixty years old, with no improvements made to them. Economically stagnant. It was true that the mountain home where Roger lived was also economically stagnant, but that was because the people enjoyed living close to the land, and rural societies were naturally stagnant and conservative. But the stagnation of suburban Prince George's County seemed at odds with the purpose of suburbia. The people could not have wanted to live in a land of rundown buildings. But that was what Roger saw from his truck.

Roger was out of Prince George's County a half hour later, drove through Anne Arundel County, and neared the city of Annapolis. Just over the Severn River Bridge, four miles before the Chesapeake Bay Bridge, the traffic stopped to a crawl. Long lines of cars crept at two miles per hour. Edge up and stop. Edge up and stop. The red of brake lights and taillights dominated the horizon. Being stuck in traffic was miserable and mind-numbing. Roger realized that he had a great urge to urinate. Two large coffees and a beer will do that. How could people stand these long traffic waits in order to cross a bridge? But the drivers seemed to be resigned to their fate. There was little obvious anger, no blowing on horns, very little cutting off of drivers. It was four miles of edge up and stop. Edge up and stop.

Half an hour of stop and go and a McDonald's beckoned. Roger cut to the right lane and exited the highway. He pulled into the McDonald's parking lot, parked, went inside a very crowded restaurant, noticed a bad smell about the inside of the building, and used the men's room. A pungent mix of urine and feces filled the bathroom, and Roger tried to relieve himself as quickly as possible. Nature taken care of, Roger left the restaurant. Usually, Roger felt obligated to buy something from a business when he used their restroom facilities, but he decided against it in this case. McDonald's had specialized in poor-quality food for many decades now, and he didn't want to reward McDonald's by buying any of their food or drinks. Any feeling of guilt was erased by the foul smell that emanated from the restaurant. Roger left the McDonald's parking lot and made for the sea of cars and trucks.

And Roger was back in the three-laned pack edging its way to the Chesapeake Bay Bridge. The rain remained steady. Finally there was a rightish curve in the highway, and the Chesapeake Bay Bridge appeared. The bridge rose from the western lip of the bay high over the choppy water. Roger could see that the bridge ran straight for a short while and then curved left as it elevated. The eastbound span of the bridge was two-laned, but overhead signs signaled one green *O* for go and one red *X* indicating a closed lane. So this was why the bridge traffic was backed up. Eastbound drivers were fighting for ground to cut over to the one open lane, and the drivers became more aggressive in jostling for position. Drivers were brazenly cutting other drivers off to get an edge to the single lane. Rudeness was a virtue if it got you closer to the one lane that got you onto the bridge. Roger was cut off twice before he adapted to the situation and became more aggressive himself.

"F—off, you West Virginia asshole," yelled an angry, stupid-looking young tough when Roger wouldn't let the man cut in front of him. Roger could hear the young man although his window was still rolled up. The young man gave Roger a middle finger, blared his horn, and then cut in front of the driver behind Roger. Success.

Roger persevered. He pulled out a beer from the cooler. If you were trapped in traffic, you might as well get the best out of wasted time. Edge and stop. Edge and stop. An 18-wheeler cut Roger off as Roger opened his beer, taking advantage of the two seconds when Roger's mind was not on the traffic. The trucker earned his advantage. Roger felt anger, got rid of his anger just as quickly, and then settled back into crossing the bridge and drink his newly poured beer. The beer was fine. The traffic remained *edge and stop*. Edge and stop. Edge and stop. And hundreds of taillights ahead taunted him.

Half an hour after his visit to McDonald's, Roger was in a single-file lane driving over the bridge. The cars and trucks and 18-wheelers motored slowly over the bridge, but progress was being made. The rain was slowing now. Roger looked quickly to his left and saw that the westbound span's traffic was moving at a brisk pace.

Eastbound traffic slowed a bit as the bridge rose to a peak above the bay but picked up as the bridge began to descend toward the Eastern Shore. Speed climbed to ten miles per hour and then twenty. Soon the ordeal was over. An hour to get to the bridge and then a ten-minute trip to get off the bridge and onto the solid ground of the Eastern Shore. What a way to live.

The shopping centers and strip malls of Kent Island were soon left behind, and Roger was now driving through the rural flatlands of the Eastern Shore. The land here was rarely ten feet above sea level. This part of Maryland was a land of grainfields of corn, soybeans, wheat, oats, hay, and barley with substantial forests in the mix. Handsome farmhouses from the distant past stood on these affluent acres of land. The crops had been harvested, and many cornfields were cut to stubble. The fields were the yellow of fall.

Easton and its shopping centers and fast-food restaurants and gas stations were passed, an ugly scar on the rural landscape. But once you were out of Easton's commercial strip, you were back into the rural heart of the Eastern Shore. Other than the flatness of the terrain, the Eastern Shore had some similarities to where Roger lived in the mountains. Both the mountains and the flatlands were rural worlds. Farms predominated. Churches were more prevalent. So were graveyards. People sold produce and homemade preserves and honey from stands and shacks at the side of the road.

And then Roger came upon Cambridge as he drove off the bridge on the Choptank River. Ugly Cambridge with boarded-up shopping centers and closed restaurants and abandoned gas stations. Even from the highway, Cambridge had a rundown feel to it. Roger's turn toward the crab country of the Eastern Shore would certainly come soon. Roger began looking for a sign for Route 16 as he passed the Cambridge McDonald's. Roger had viewed a map of Maryland the night before and knew he had to find Route 16 west to get into the crab country. There it was. Roger saw the black sign for Route 16 as he sped up to a Walmart opposite what seemed to Roger to be a resort or hotel of some kind. Roger turned right and drove southwest toward crab country. He first passed through the slums of south Cambridge with its two-story bungalows and scores of Black children running about and some on bikes hurtling about, laughing at each other's daring and prowess. Older Blacks sat on chairs on their front stoops watching the world go by and enjoying each other's company. Some of the teenaged girls had babies on their laps. But within a couple minutes Roger was clean out of Cambridge and into a world very much different than the small-town squalor of Cambridge.

The new world Roger entered was one of an occasional farm of corn, soybeans, or sorghum; brackish coves; thick pinewoods; small motor boats; produce stands; crab traps stacked on front yards; and comfortable homes with short piers, back decks, and picnic tables. The pinewoods lay out as far as the eye could see and ran down to the inlets and coves. It was marshy and tidal, and an occasional dead fish bobbed up and down near the shore. Herons flew about from one fetch of water to another, looking for a meal. Canadian geese in checkmark formation neared Roger as he drove and landed in a field of cornstalk stubble. This flatland was much different than the land of the mountains but had its own wonder about it. It was close to nature. This flatland of the Eastern Shore had a splendor that the suburban dystopia Roger had passed through in the morning could never have.

At a small bridge that crossed a tidal creek, a man and two boys were fishing. The man was middle-aged, smoking a cigar and drinking a can of beer. The two boys looked to be in their early teens, and their fishing tackle sat in a heap at the left side of the bridge. The boys were laughing as they held their rods. On the right-hand side of the bridge was a boat ramp parallel to the bridge. A small wiry man in a small skiff chugged up to the landing with a small stag lying in the front of the skiff. It was dead, shot clean through its neck. As Roger slowed his truck to a crawl, the man fishing with his boys called out to the hunter in the skiff, and the hunter grinned and replied to the other man.

Roger pulled over to a gravel parking lot near the ramp and got out of the truck. He walked over to the hunter as the hunter was securing the boat to a pole next to the ramp.

"Nice deer," said Roger as he reached the ramp. The sun was high in the sky now, the rain was gone, and the day was beautiful.

The hunter looked up from the skiff and said, "Thanks." Although he was small, the hunter looked reliant and purposeful. The man's face was weathered and reddish, and he wore a baseball cap that was heavily stained. The cap was green and in black letters spelled out the name of a local plumbing company, Pusey and Sons. A black crossbow sat in the middle of the skiff. "A sika deer. I nailed him on the island," said the hunter, and he pointed in the distance toward his left. The hunter tied another line to a pole and pulled himself out of the skiff. He walked over to where his pickup truck and trailer were parked in the gravel, got into his truck, and backed it up to the skiff. The skiff was trailered in three minutes, and the hunter drove the skiff onto the parking lot, where it dripped with water. The hunter got out of his truck and lit a cigarette.

"You look like you do this often," said Roger.

"Yep. I love archery season. I like it better than rifle. Something more personal about killing a deer with a bow instead of a rifle. Yeah, it is more personal."

"I've always hunted with a rifle, never with a bow. I imagine the range of a bow is much less," said Roger.

"Sure. That's why hunting with a bow is more of a challenge. You have to get closer to your mark." The hunter smiled.

"How close were you to the deer? Sika, you called it."

"Thirty yards, I guess."

"Is the sika deer native to this area?"

"No. About a hundred years ago some fella introduced them to one of the islands on the bay. I forget which one. They bred really well and eventually got off the island. They really take to the woods and marshes around here. They really go after the soybeans and corn for their food source. They like to munch on bayberries too. You know, the sikas aren't really deer. They're part of the elk family. From the Orient. Japan, mostly."

"I didn't know that. To be honest, I've never heard of the sika deer. I'm a mountain boy from West Virginia."

"That so? Far from home."

"Yep. My wife is from around here. I haven't been here for years. My wife's kin kind of died off or moved away from the Eastern Shore."

"That so. This used to be a great place to live. You could live pretty much in freedom even if the taxes were so sky high. But the state government don't like folks like us. People of the Eastern Shore are very much in the minority in this state. Baltimore city and the Washington suburbs run the state and country folks that live on the Shore are jack shit to them. The Shore is just a place to pass through to get to the beach for vacation. I dare say that we're an oddity on the Shore, like animals in a zoo."

"Sorry to hear that. Where I live, the problem isn't the local or state government. We live pretty free. Every house has a gun, and most have several. The police don't plan on taking away our guns. They wouldn't and couldn't. But we are fearful of the national government. With the Supreme Court virtually abolishing the Second Amendment, we wonder what the feds have up their sleeves."

"Ain't that a fact."

Roger got back into his truck and drove off. It must have been past noon. The sun was high in the sky. He passed an old Methodist church and graveyard with raised vaults. Weeds had overtaken much of the graveyard, and the church was ramshackle and its white paint was peeling badly. Across from the church were two abandoned houses. The one house was two-storied, and all its windows were knocked out and the roof over the front porch was half collapsed into the porch. The second house was small and had a porch that had been screened, but its screens were all ripped up. The front door did not exist so that the house was open.

Further down the road ahead of Roger, a rafter of wild turkeys ran across the pavement from one side of woods to another. Roger slowed the truck down to let the wild turkeys pass. One of the turkeys was a tom with a red head and throat, and he was much bigger than the other turkeys. The tom was bearded and in full glory.

Ten minutes driving through heavy pinewoods, Roger approached a cluster of buildings in an opening in the woods. Toward the front was a large residence of brick, and it had two stories. Roger turned into a long, paved driveway and passed the big house. The driveway became a lot of oyster shells after he passed the house. One of the buildings in the rear was a small white commercial building with a sign that said *Blanton's*. Farther in the rear was a large metallic building that looked like a small factory. Steam wisped from a vent at the right side of the building. That must be where the crabs were processed. Roger found it curious that the parking lot was empty of cars or trucks. He stepped out of his truck and walked over to the small commercial building and turned the doorknob. It was locked. He knocked on the door, but there was no answer. How strange that a business that sold crab would be closed at this time of day.

A man in a crumpled suit walked Roger's way from a doorway at the crab processing plant. He was a short man with a flinty face, and he wore a scowl. He had jet-black hair combed away from his ugly face, and he was missing teeth. The man had the build of a boxer who had stopped training many years before. He may have been fifty years of age.

"What the hell are you snooping about?" he asked as he strode up to Roger.

"I wanted to buy some crab. Why are you closed?"

"We ain't commercial no more. Haven't been for two years. Everyone 'round here knows about it. Except for you." The man tapped his meaty right fist against his left.

"I'm not from around here. I drove here on a day trip from the mountains. I last came here years ago and always liked the scenery. And the crab."

The man snickered. "You picked a bad time for a day trip. Ain't no crab to be bought. And you like the scenery? You sound like a f——ing tourist. This place you think has scenery is really a dump. I can't stand the place, to put it bluntly. I only came here for a job. Scenery my ass." He spat on the ground.

"So you're not from around here?" Roger asked.

"Hell, no. Don't like it here. There's no action here like back in the city. I don't like quiet. I like things loud. But I needed a job, so I took this one working for the government overseeing this property."

"So the government is in the crab business?" Roger asked.

60

The man looked at Roger harshly and shook his head disdainfully. "What are you getting at? That's not the sort of question people should be asking. Are you some kind of wise guy?"

Roger smiled. "I just find it strange that the crab-processing plant seems to be in full operation, but I don't see any cars or trucks or people other than yourself. And I can't buy any crab." Roger pointed at the plant.

"What happens in that g—damned plant is none of your f—king business. Why don't you just beat it? Get your ass back in your g—damned pickup truck and get the hell out of here. What happens in the plant is none of your f—king business. Got it, gray hair?" The man motioned his right thumb like a baseball umpire.

"Glad to be gone," Roger replied, and he drove off.

Three miles down the road was a general store with a couple of cars parked in a small lot. Roger pulled in, parked, and went inside. The front of the store consisted of four long rows of mostly snack foods, a few canned goods, and a few automobile supplies. At the left of the front door was a corner with two cash registers. Toward the right wall and the back wall of the store were refrigerated sodas and beer. At the left rear of the store was an older fat woman wearing a white apron at a small grill, chatting with a younger, heavyset woman wearing pajamas and eating what looked to be a breakfast sandwich. A small black chalkboard on the wall behind the cook had a list of sandwiches handwritten in white.

Roger walked past the rows of goods and toward the grill. He hadn't eaten yet and was hungry. He looked over the list of sandwiches on the chalkboard for a minute as the two women stopped talking and looked him over. Roger asked the cook, "What is scrapple?"

The cook gave Roger a puzzled look and laughed. "Hey, you ain't from around here, son. What ya doin? Touring? We don't get many tourists round here. Tourists usually like places like St. Michaels. Did you take a wrong turn?"

"No. I came here on purpose. My wife grew up in these parts."

"She did? Good for her," the fat cook replied with a snicker. "Where is she?"

"She's dead."

"Oh. I'm sorry. Sad to hear it. I'm sorry."

"So what's in scrapple?" Roger asked.

"Everything leftover from a pig that hasn't been made into sausage, bacon, or ham. Ears. Noses. Testicles too." The cook guffawed loudly, and the young woman giggled, a piece of sandwich flying out of her mouth.

"Give me a scrapple-and-egg sandwich, please."

"On what? Bread or English muffin?"

"English muffin would be fine."

The cook walked over to a small refrigerator along the wall, pulled out a loaf of scrapple, and cut it off a piece with a knife. She flicked the scrapple onto a hot grill, wiped the knife off on her apron, and placed the knife on a small table next to the grill. The scrapple began to sizzle.

"How do you want your egg, mister?" asked the cook.

"Over easy."

"Okay." The cook reached into the refrigerator and pulled out an egg.

A minute went by. Roger heard the front door open and shut, and he could hear a man speaking with a woman at the cash register. The cook flipped the scrapple with a plastic spatula and began to cook the egg on the other side of the grill.

"I tried to buy some crab down at a place called Blanton's and couldn't get any," said Roger. "Why's that?"

The cook looked away, and the younger woman looked down at the floor. They said nothing, but their silence told Roger that they knew more than what they chose not to reveal. Was he asking them to reveal a state secret?

The man who had entered the store walked the floor and over to the grill. He was in his thirties and wore black rubber hip waders, blue jeans, a ratty red-and-black checkered flannel shirt, and a black windbreaker. His face was heavily tanned as if he worked outside most of the time. His brown hair was uncombed. The man was muscular but not tall. His eyes were sky blue.

"I'll tell you, mister. The government has requisitioned all the crabmeat," said the man. The two women looked at the man and just as quickly looked away at the floor.

"How can they do that?" asked Roger.

"Because they can," answered the man gruffly.

"Seems odd. Un-American," said Roger.

"That so? Seems odd to me too," said the man. "There's talk that big shots want it all in Washington and New York. To make sure all the fancy restaurants have enough crabmeat for their fancy hundred-dollar-a-plate meals. That's the talk, anyway." The cook handed Roger a sandwich on a small white paper plate, and Roger sat down at a small plastic table.

"Are you a crabber?" asked Roger. The cook rolled her eyes, but the man smiled.

"Yeah. I'm a waterman. I have to sell my catch at set prices to government agents that lurk all about every dock on the Shore."

"Set prices. Doesn't seem to be free market."

"Nah. The government tells you what the market is. Right now, it's hard to make money in crabs," replied the waterman with a shake of his head.

"Any black market?" Roger asked.

"Don't say them words, mister. People can get in trouble saying those words. They can even get killed. Yes, sir. The government wants no black market. That's why we have all the snoops down at the docks."

"I guess you can tell one when you see one."

"Of course. They don't know nothing about crabs other than they want all the crab at their prices. Everybody knows who these bastards are. But we go around pretending that we don't know who they are when we damned well know who they are. Rats."

"Two of them moved into a house just up the road from me," interjected the cook. "Black Mercedes car. DC plates. They keep to themselves."

"The crab-processing plants. Are they government run?" asked Roger.

"No. The same people who ran them before requisitioning run them now. The government is too damned dumb to actually run a business operation," said the waterman with a chuckle. The two women chuckled along. "But you can be damned sure that the plants are crawling with agents."

"I think I ran into one at Blanton's. He gave me a hard time."

"You tried to buy crab?" asked the waterman and he smiled broadly.

"Yeah."

"You're crazy. The requisition law has been the law for about two years now. Everybody around here knows about it. Hell, he might have thought you were going to contact a picker and get some black-market jumbo lump. There's a lot of money in black-market jumbo lump and not enough agents to crack down on everyone, I have been told," said the waterman with a roll of his eyes.

"Jumbo lump is traded like gold," said the cook. "Heard it can go for one hundred bucks for a pound of jumbo lump, even more. Just got to know the right waterman," the cook finished with a chuckle.

"Don't say that, Liz. You know us watermen are absolutely honest and respectful of the government," answered the waterman with a laugh. Roger and the two women laughed with the waterman. The waterman continued. "With all them agents at the docks, it'd really hard to sneak any crab off the boats. There's more black-market crab to be had at the plants. That's because the pickers are a shifty lot, and most don't speak English very good."

"Or not at all," the cook broke in.

"Can't speak English. Where are they from?" Roger asked.

"Mexico," the waterman replied. "Mexicans and others from south of the border have done almost all the crab pickin' for years. They work cheap. They go all day pickin' crabs and don't complain, at least not in English. White folks have better ways to make money. Blacks don't do that sort of work anymore. But because the Mexicans no *comprende Englais*, they can get away with a lot of things. Even with cameras all over the plants. You can watch them real hard, but even the government agents can't catch 'em all the time."

The younger woman spoke. "They use their kids to smuggle crab out. It's said that they'll even drop a bag of jumbo lump down a little girl's panties or a baby's diaper. Whose gonna check? Even the agents don't want to check to see if a lump in the diaper is jumbo lump crab instead of a load of shit." The two women, the waterman, and Roger laughed.

"The agents let the beaners get away with small-scale chicken-shit smugglin," said the waterman. "All the Mexicans do it, and even if they caught 'em all, who's is gonna pick the crab? Not Americans. You hear that they occasionally crack down on big smugglin' operations. A family named Martinez who worked at Hooper's was smugglin' hundreds of pounds at a time. The agents caught 'em. But the word is that they dropped the charges. Why did they do so? They were Hispanics. The government considers Hispanics to be a protected people. You can't prosecute minorities, you see."

"Ain't that the truth," said Liz.

"Once crab gets on the trucks, it's hard to steal the crab. The trucks are still owned by the plants, and the drivers are people from around here. But the agents ride shotgun with the trucks. Armed agents. Sidearms. Dark-blue uniforms with police hats. And there's cameras in every truck. So the trucks don't get hijacked. Too hard. Sometimes you even get a police escort. It used to be that you rarely saw federal police on the Shore. Not anymore. The Shore is crawling with fed cops. And the Maryland state troopers help out too. The Maryland politicians all support the feds, and that's a fact. So the state troopers are guard dogs for the federal government."

"How do the people who actually live here think about the feds?' Roger asked.

The waterman looked harshly at Roger and said, "How would you feel if the way of life you lived your lives for as long as anyone remembered got changed because some government workers in DC decided to change your lives? We hate it. And we hate them." The two women shook their heads.

"I can't remember the last time I ate crab soup," said Liz.

"Me neither," said the younger woman. "At least two years since I had a bowl of crab soup. I miss a bowl of crab soup on a cold winter's day."

"Can you imagine," said the waterman, "that with all the crab caught here on the Chesapeake, few people are able to eat it. When they do, it costs an arm and a leg. In the midst of plenty, we get screwed out of our crabmeat, mister."

"And we're taught that we live in the land of the free. Doesn't seem that way, no how," said Liz.

The waterman looked at Roger intently and said, "You know, mister, that you were on camera when you stopped to buy crab at Blanton's? Probably got your plates, and those West Virginia plates will stand out, I am pretty sure. You see, that security man at Blanton's probably got in touch with some sort of superior once he got rid of you. Nobody around here is dumb enough to think Blanton's sells any crabmeat. The government probably knows who you are and where you're from by now."

"You think?"

"I'm not all knowing. But I have my hunch. I believe the authorities who run the crab racket find you to be a mighty interesting person. Coming to the Shore from some mountain in West Virginia. That's unknown to happen these days. Yep. I'd say they might think you're a threat, some sort of criminal threat. That's how paranoid the government is. You look like a regular sort of guy minding his own business. Just wanted to buy some crabmeat."

"I don't feel like an animal or a criminal. I just think of myself as a free man."

"There ain't no free men anymore," said the waterman. "As for being criminals, we're all potential criminals according to the government."

"Hey, what you want to eat, Tim?" asked Liz, and she slapped the spatula in her right hand against the grill.

"I've been working all morning. I could use a cheeseburger with a couple of pieces of bacon on it," the waterman replied.

"You know that's not on the menu," said Liz. "Read the board." She pointed at the chalkboard.

"Come on now, Liz. It's afternoon. You just haven't changed your board, girl. Get that bacon going, and make me a big old cheeseburger."

Roger finished his sandwich and rose from the table. He looked at Liz. "Thanks for the sandwich. It tasted really fine."

"You're welcome, stranger," Liz replied. "Pay at the register."

Roger looked at the waterman who had just sat at the small table where the younger woman sat. "Thanks for the information. And thanks for the warning."

"No problem," said the waterman. "Best of luck to you."

Roger paid the woman at the register, left the store, and stepped into his truck and drove toward Cambridge. He reached into his cooler and pulled out a beer, opened it, and poured it into his travel cup. It tasted good. The piney woods thinned out, and ten minutes after leaving the store Roger was driving through the same slums he had passed through earlier in the day. Bluish lights showed in his rearview mirror. It was a police car thirty yards behind Roger. *Must be an emergency, the cop couldn't be for me.* The cop sped faster, and he was close behind Roger. The cop was for Roger. Roger pulled off to the side of the road, placed his travel cup in the cooler in the back seat, put his flashers on, and placed his two hands on the steering wheel. Roger looked through his rearview window. The police car stopped behind him. There was a thirty-second wait, and the cop got out of his car. From the rearview mirror, Roger could tell that the cop was short, young, and white. The cop strode up to Roger's truck, flashlight in his left hand, and tapped the driver's side window. Roger dutifully rolled the window down and handed the cop his driver's license.

"Do you know why I stopped you?" asked the policeman.

"No, officer," Roger answered.

"Your tag light is out. Not a problem now but it will be at night." The cop looked at Roger closely, and he sniffed. "Sir, have you been drinking?"

Dread ran through Roger's mind. Do I tell the truth? Or just enough truth to get by? He knows that I have been drinking, and cops don't like to be lied to. That's always a mistake. Can the cop see the cooler behind the front seat? Of course he can unless he's a damned fool. But he's young and inexperienced. Perhaps he doesn't see the cooler.

"I've had two beers today, officer," Roger lied. He had really had four. Or was it five?

The policeman looked at Roger. He asked, "Do you mind turning off your vehicle and stepping out of your truck, sir?"

"No." Roger turned off the truck. The cop stepped back to allow Roger to get out. Roger opened the door and got out.

"Would you please walk back to the rear of your truck?" asked the cop.

"Sure." Roger followed the cop to the rear of the truck.

"Would you stand next to the bumper of your truck?"

"Sure."

"Do you have any physical impediments that would prevent you from performing a series of exercises?"

"Not really. I'm fifty-seven years old, but I'm in pretty good shape. No, officer. No impediments."

"Fine."

"Please say the numbers fifty on down to forty inclusive, and then say them back again back up to fifty," said the cop.

Roger began. "Fifty. Forty-nine. Forty-eight. Forty-seven. Forty-six. Forty-five. Forty-four. Forty-three. Forty-two. Forty-one. Forty. Forty-one. Forty-two. Forty-three. Forty-four. Forty-five. Forty-six. Forty-seven. Forty-eight. Forty-nine. Fifty." Easy. Roger had drunk some beer but wasn't drunk.

The cop pulled a pen from his shirt pocket and held it three feet from Roger's face. "Do you see the pen?" the cop asked.

"Yes."

"Follow the pen as I motion it," ordered the cop.

The cop moved the pen slowly to Roger's left and reversed course to Roger's right. Roger's peripheral vision was very good, so he didn't have to turn his head to follow the pen.

The cop glared at Roger and said, "You're trying to cheat the test. I'll take you in right now if you continue to try to cheat the test." Roger noticed another police car pull up. It was a Maryland state trooper's car. A tall, athletic trooper, military in bearing, stepped out of his car and began to walk toward Roger and the cop.

"I'm not trying to cheat any test, officer. What am I doing wrong?"

"You know what you're doing wrong."

"No, I don't officer."

"You're not moving your head with the motion of the pen."

"I didn't know that was the purpose of the test. I have very good side-to-side vision. I didn't need to move my head to follow the pen."

"You've taken this test before, right?" the cop asked.

"No. I've only been stopped for speeding and not for drinking."

"So follow my pen with your head and eyes."

"All right."

The cop moved his pen to Roger's right, then to his left, and then back to his right. Roger made sure to move his head with the pen in the cop's hand.

"Okay," said the cop with mild disgust. The state trooper stopped walking and stood about thirty feet away and watched.

"Now I want you to hold your right leg in the air at a forty-five-degree angle and count one Mississippi, two Mississippi, and so forth until I tell you to stop. Understand?"

"Yeah." Roger raised his right leg and angled it two feet from the cop. "One Mississippi. Two Mississippi. Three Mississippi. Four Mississippi. Five Mississippi. Six Mississippi. Seven Mississippi. Eight Mississippi. Nine Mississippi. Ten Mississippi." The Maryland state trooper slowly walked forward closer to Roger and the cop. Significant? "Eleven Mississippi. Twelve Mississippi. Thirteen Mississippi. Fourteen Mississippi. Fifteen Mississippi. Sixteen Mississippi. Seventeen Mississippi. Eighteen Mississippi." Roger's leg was beginning to tire and feel sore, but he continued. "Nineteen Mississippi. Twenty Mississippi. Twenty-one Mississippi. Twenty-two Mississippi. Twenty-three Mississippi. Twenty-four Mississippi."

"All right. That's enough. You can put your leg down," the cop ordered. The cop walked back to his car, briefly spoke with the trooper, and reached for something in the back of his car. Roger couldn't tell what it was yet. The cop walked back toward where Roger stood, passing the trooper. The trooper followed five steps behind. In the cop's left hand was a small black device with a white tube attached. Some sort of breathalyzer.

"Sir, do you mind blowing into this device?" asked the cop.

"No, officer."

The cop held the breathalyzer to Roger's face. The white tube dangled from the breathalyzer inches away from Roger's mouth. Roger was nervous. Four beers or was it five? Did five beers in five hours ring you up with an .08? He would find out in a moment.

"Sir, would you please blow into the tube? You don't have to but, if you don't, I'll have to take you down to the station."

Roger put the tube in his mouth. Nerves getting the better of him, Roger inhaled strongly rather than exhaling. The trooper called out angrily, "Blow!" And Roger reversed his action. He exhaled strongly into the white tube, and the cop got a reading. Roger could see some blue numbers, but the cop angled the numbers in a way that Roger could not see them. The cop showed the breathalyzer to the trooper, and the trooper appeared disappointed.

The cop walked back to where Roger stood. "All right," he said. He showed Roger the reading. It read .066. "Pretty high but not enough to bring you in." A third police car pulled up on the side of the road. The cop continued. "But I will have to write you up on that tag light. You can go ahead and wait in your truck. It'll take me a few minutes."

Roger got back into his truck. He felt a great wave of relief. The trooper walked over to Roger's truck and looked about. He was sure to see the small cooler behind the driver's seat. The trooper was not some callow youth but an experienced policeman. The trooper looked through the driver's window. Roger and the seat blocked the view to the cooler behind. The trooper circled to the passenger window. He was sure to see the cooler now. Do they arrest for open containers in Maryland? Or was it a fine and points? Then again, there wasn't an actual container open in the front seat, only a container with half a beer in the cooler. Can't a man drive his truck with a cooler of beer in the state of Maryland? Roger was sure he would find out in a few seconds. The trooper stared into the window for what seemed to Roger to be at least ten seconds. Roger knew the trooper would figure things out and that he had a cooler of beer and a travel cup with half a beer in it. But then the trooper walked away, his face stone.

The newly arrived policeman strode past the trooper's car and the cop's car. He met the trooper halfway in front of the cop's car, and they spoke. The young town cop stepped out of his car and walked over to Roger's truck with a black ticket book in his left hand. He reached the window, ripped out Roger's ticket, and handed the ticket to Roger.

"Mr. Lee, you have a month to conduct repairs to your tag light. When you do, you can either bring your ticket to a Maryland state trooper's barracks and have the truck inspected and signed, and then you can mail it in, or you can have your repair shop sign the ticket that says they completed the needed repairs to your vehicle and mail it with a copy of the receipt of the work performed on your truck. Do you understand?"

"Yeah, I understand. I'll get the tag light repaired right away and mail it in."

"Fine," said the cop.

"Am I free to drive on?" asked Roger.

"Yes. You may leave, Mr. Lee," replied the cop and he walked away. Roger rolled up the truck window.

Roger was about to turn on the ignition when the third policeman walked up to Roger's window. The trooper was trailing, and the young cop had turned around and was walking back toward Roger.

The third policeman tapped on Roger's window with a nightstick. Roger rolled down the window. "Not so fast," ordered the third policeman. "Do not turn on your vehicle. Place both hands on the steering wheel," he said severely. "What is it that you have stuck to your rear bumper?"

"What do you mean?"

"Just answer the question." The policeman was a solidly built man and had the body of a fullback. He was about thirty and wore a blondish buzz cut. His policeman blue cap read *Department of Interior Security* in gold letters.

"I don't know. Maybe a bumper sticker, I suppose."

"And what do the letters CSA mean?" asked the policeman.

"What do they mean? Why do you ask?"

"I'm asking the questions here, mister. Your duty is to answer any questions I ask, got it?" said the policeman, steel in his tone. The trooper and the young cop continued to walk toward Roger's truck. What was this all about? "Repeat," said the policeman. "What do the letters CSA mean?"

"Confederate States of America."

"Thought so. Are you some sort of rebel? Some sort of malcontent?"

"No."

"And that's the Confederate flag that's part of the bumper sticker, right?"

"Yes. It is the Confederate battle flag."

The trooper and the cop reached Roger's truck. The policeman slowly wheeled and said, "We have a problem here. This man," and he pointed at Roger, "is a potential security risk to our government. He'll have to be arrested and be questioned further."

The policeman turned his head toward Roger and said, "Mister, you will step out of your truck?"

"What's this all about?" asked Roger. "Are bumper stickers now illegal?"

"Certain bumper stickers tell us about the security risks of an individual. Your bumper sticker tells me that you are a potential risk and possibly a deplorable."

"Deplorable?"

"Yes. Now step out of your truck as ordered," said the policeman.

"Sure," Roger answered, resigned to submit to authority. He stepped out of the truck.

The policeman looked over at the town cop and said, "Take this man to the city station and begin the process of booking him. I'll follow you." He looked at the trooper. "I guess you can go. I think we're all set here."

"Sir, please come to the back of your truck and place your hands on the tailgate," said the town cop. Roger did so. "Place your hands on the tailgate," the town cop repeated. Roger complied. The cop frisked Roger and felt Roger's keys and wallet. The cop grabbed the handcuffs at his waist, grabbed Roger's right hand, and pulled it to the small of Roger's back. The cop did the same with Roger's left hand. The cop led Roger by the left arm to his police car, opened the left rear door, and guided Roger to a seat.

A heavy glass divider separated Roger from the cop. Both side windows and the rear window had bars embedded in the glass. The cop drove off, followed by the security policeman. Within five minutes the two cars arrived at a large block building with a metal sliding gate. The two cars passed through the gate and were at the back door of the police station in seconds.

The cop led Roger into the police station. A policeman was on the other side of the door at the security desk. The cop said to the policeman at the security desk, "I'm taking him to booking." The cop led Roger down a well-lit hallway. It was a short hallway, and the two men took a sharp left turn into a rather large room. A sign at the back of the room said *Booking*. A large cream-colored table was centered in the room. A heavy glass bulwark bisected the table, but it was low enough that the booker and the person being booked could speak easily to each other. On one side of the table was a simple wooden chair. On the other side of the table sat a black laptop computer with a cushioned chair for the policeman to sit. The cop uncuffed Roger.

"Before you sit down," ordered the cop, "take out your wallet and keys and give them to me." Roger handed the cop his wallet and keys. "Any change, give it to me." Roger gave the cop a few coins from his left pants' pocket. The cop pulled out a bucket and tossed the wallet, keys, and coins in the bucket. "Your belt, take it off." Roger unbuckled his belt, pulled it off, and gave it to the cop. An older cop came in through a door at the far end of the room and looked through a file cabinet. The older cop was a blockheaded man, pudgy, and balding with dull brown eyes. He was about fifty and had the face of a basset hound. "Take off your shoes and give them to me," the cop continued. Roger unlaced his shoes and gave the shoes to the cop. The cop pointed at the chair. "All right. Sit down."

"What is your full name?" asked the cop.

"Roger Hardin Lee."

"Do you spell Roger with a *d* or not?

"No *d*."

"Hardin and Lee. Normal spelling?"

"Yes. Normal spelling.

"What is your address?"

"Forty-five Wilkins Farm Road, Stonewall, West Virginia."

"*Stonewall,* two words or one?"

"One."

"Named after a wall?"

"No. It is named after a general."

"A general? Hmm. Which war?"

"The Civil War."

"Oh. Way back."

"Right. A long time ago."

"Height?"

"Five-eleven."

"Weight?"

"One seventy-five."

"Hair color?"

"It used to be brown. Now it's pretty gray and white. Goes with my age."

"How old are you?"

"Fifty-seven."

"Date of birth?"

"May 12, 1978."

"Any record? We can look it up, you know."

"A couple of speeding tickets. That's it. I've never been arrested."

"Good for you."

"Married?"

"No. My wife died. I'm a widower."

Three cops came in through a side door. Two were Black men. One was gangly and young and wore his black hair slicked back from his forehead. The other Black policeman was older and roundish and looked like he would have a difficult job running down any suspect. The other cop was a young white woman of stocky frame. She was short, wore her auburn hair cut very short, and looked as unathletic as the older Black cop. The three of them were laughing as each sat down at tables on the far side of the room. The blockheaded cop finished looking through the files, traded greetings with the three cops who had just entered the room, and left.

The town cop had Roger walk over to where a camera sat on a desk. Three photos—front, left side, and right side—were taken of Roger's face. Then he was fingerprinted. The cop led Roger back to the big table where the booking process had begun. The cop tapped away at the computer for several minutes. The security policeman who had been instrumental in Roger's arrest came in from the back of the room and stood quietly as the town cop typed on the laptop. This went on for a couple minutes until the cop stopped typing.

"No outstanding warrants. Speeding ticket in 2028. You're clean. But today you are being charged with being a danger to national security," said the town cop. The security policeman nodded and shot a mean smirk Roger's way. "Stand and come this way," said the town cop, and the two men went to a door at the end of the room. The security cop did not walk with the other two men. The cop opened the door and led Roger through the door. On the other side of the door was the blockheaded cop and a simple heavy plastic bench. The room was small and dingy, with two cameras on the wall. The blockheaded cop handed the young cop a plastic bucket.

"Please remove all of your clothing. You can use the bench to sit on if you like," said the blockheaded cop to Roger.

"Why is this necessary?" asked Roger.

"For your safety and our safety. If you have contraband, we don't want you to get it into our jail. Anyway, having illegal contraband is a crime in itself," said the blockheaded cop.

"This is crazy," said Roger. "My crime is having a politically incorrect bumper sticker, and I'm being booked, charged, and strip-searched. This is madness."

The blockheaded cop grinned. "First, you're not charge—yet. As for you thinking this is madness, it may seem like madness to you, but it is a process to us. Nothing more. We process you because the internal security police have reason to suspect that you are a security risk. When an arrest becomes a process rather than a personal action between the police and suspect, it becomes easier to perform." The blockheaded cop paused. "So please take off your clothes. All of them. You're going to do it eventually, so you might as well do it voluntarily and retain your self-respect."

"I don't see how I can retain my self-respect voluntarily taking my clothes off in front of two men," Roger shot back.

The blockheaded cop put on a pair of transparent plastic gloves. "Sir, let's make this as easy as possible on all of us. All arrested suspects are strip-searched upon being incarcerated. It is how we do things here, and most jurisdictions do it as we do. It is not like we enjoy strip-searching a man," said the blockheaded cop.

Roger sat on the bench and began to undress. Shirt. Blue jeans. Underwear. Socks. He stood, and the young cop held out the bucket, and Roger dropped his clothes into the bucket. Roger was standing there in front of two policemen totally naked, and he felt cold and shook slightly.

"What is that brown string around your neck? With the two square patches?" asked the blockheaded cop, pointing at Roger.

"My scapular." Roger had forgotten that he was wearing it.

"What the hell is that?" asked the blockheaded cop with a chuckle.

"A scapular is a religious item for Catholics to wear."

"A religious item, huh?" said the blockheaded cop.

"Yes. We Catholics believe we receive indulgences from God for wearing the scapular."

The blockheaded cop laughed. "Sort of like a good-luck charm. Never heard of a scapular." The blockheaded cop looked at the young cop. "Did you ever hear of a scapular, Officer Tillman?"

"No. Never have. But I'm sure they're not allowed in the jail. A suspect might hang himself with it," answered Officer Tillman.

"All right. Mr. suspect, give me your scapular. You can't keep it. We'll store it for you if you get out of our jail," said the blockheaded cop. "Take it off and drop it in the bucket with the rest of your gear." Roger did so.

"Please open your mouth," the blockheaded cop ordered. Roger obeyed. The blockheaded cop stuck his gloved right hand into Roger's mouth, gave Roger's mouth a three-second exam, and then proceeded to walk behind Roger.

"Please spread your legs as wide as possible and reach as far to the floor as possible."

"I doubt I can touch my toes, officer. I'm a little old."

"Just as far as you can. If you can reach your shins, that will do." The blockheaded cop felt inside Roger's ears, his armpits, down his back, and briefly in the rectal area.

"Clean," announced the blockheaded cop. The blockheaded cop reversed the plastic glove, walked over to a small plastic trash can, and threw out the glove. He then walked over to a plastic bag sitting on a small table at the left side of the room and pulled out a bright-orange jumpsuit and handed it to Roger. "Please put this suit on. Snap the buttons." Roger did as ordered. "And put these booties on." Roger slipped on two white booties on his feet.

The blockheaded cop pointed at Officer Tillman and said to Roger, "Follow Officer Tillman. The three of us will proceed down the hall to Detention Room 2, and that's where you will stay momentarily." The three men left the room, Officer Tillman leading the way, Roger next, and the blockheaded cop in the rear. The three men walked down the hall. An older policeman coming from the other direction passed them without saying a word. A second policeman appeared through a door at the end of the hall and waited for the three men at a door at the rear of the hall and to the left. This second policeman placed a small device against an electronic lock, and the door slid open. The second policeman deferentially looked at the blockheaded cop. The blockheaded cop blandly said, "Sir, we'll keep you in here for the time being. Please step inside."

The room was roughly ten feet by ten feet. It was well lit. Attached high on one of the walls was a round metallic device, which obviously was a camera. A cobalt-colored lounge sat at the far side of the room. It was eight feet long and two feet wide. A place to sit and sleep. On the lounge was a folded gray blanket. Roger walked over to the lounge and sat.

The bed was made of very hard plastic and was uncomfortable to sit on. The jumpsuit provided very little padding, and Roger's posterior was sore within minutes. He sat there a while looking ahead at the front wall and door, and he was very bored very quickly. Hospitals were tedious places most of the time, but being kept in jail was even worse. Roger questioned his situation and why he was arrested. A bumper sticker and a bad tag light got him into the jail. What a chickenshit reason to stop a man minding his own business. All on a day he just wanted to buy some crabmeat and drink some beer. Now he was in jail for having a politically incorrect bumper sticker on his car. His plight was insane.

An hour became two hours, and Roger tried to lie down on the blanket, but its padding was insufficient. The whole length of Roger's body became sore. He stood and paced. He prayed a rosary and then prayed another. The Sorrowful Mysteries first and the Glorious Mysteries after that. Did he dare say the Joyful Mysteries? He had plenty of time, so he said the Joyful Mysteries. And then he said all three again. Then he said ten Memorares. And then ten Hail, Holy Queens. Jail was a vile place to be but Roger had plenty of time to pray.

Finally, the door slid open and the blockheaded cop, the internal security cop who had him arrested for the Confederate bumper sticker, and two middle-aged men dressed in dark suits and sporting navy blue ties stepped through the doorway. One of the men was short and wiry and was beginning to bald at the front of his crown. His eyes were nearly black, two little bullets. His face was beginning to beard as it was now late in the day. He flashed a short smile, a smile without joy when he looked over at Roger. In his right hand was a laptop computer. The other man was several inches taller than Roger and stocky like a Santa Claus. He had a beaked nose, and his hair was a crew cut blond.

"Mr. Lee, please step this way," ordered the blockheaded cop. "Walk down the hall to your left." Roger stepped to his left and proceeded to walk down the hall. The four men followed. They came to another door, and the blockheaded cop used a pass card to open the door. The door slid open. Another hallway appeared, and the five men began walking down the hall. A Black policeman coming from the opposite direction passed them by, barely acknowledging the five men.

"Stop," said the blockheaded cop. They had reached a door to their right that read *Interrogation*. The blockheaded cop pulled out the pass card, and the door slid open. The blockheaded cop pointed into the room. Roger, the security cop, and the two men dressed in suits walked through the doorway and into the room, but the block-headed cop remained in the hall. The door slid shut with a metallic click.

"Sit down, Mr. Lee," said the shorter of the two suited men. He pointed to a black-cushioned chair to the left of a small table. The smaller suited man placed the laptop computer on the table, sat in a chair opposite Roger, opened up the laptop, and began typing.

"Mr. Lee, my name is Nelson." He looked over at the bigger man and pointed at him. "He is Mr. Knutson." Knutson looked blankly at the two men sitting. "You are an interesting character, Mr. Lee. Very interesting."

"I'm surprised you think so," said Roger.

"You own some sort of farm in West Virginia," said Nelson. "I've never known anyone who farmed before. What kind of farm?"

"I grow apples for the most part."

"Apples?"

"Right. Apples."

"How much money can you make selling apples?"

"Not a whole lot. But I don't need a lot of money. It's cheap to live in the mountains. And I don't believe in debt, so I don't spend a lot of money."

"No mortgage at all?"

"No. I'm free. Totally free. Except for right now." Nelson scowled and bore two rows of short teeth.

"Why is a man from the West Virginia mountains visiting the Eastern Shore of Maryland?" asked Nelson.

"To buy crabmeat." Roger noticed that the security policeman rolled his eyes and then shook his head.

"Crabmeat?" said Knutson. He chortled without mirth.

"Yes. Crabmeat," said Roger.

"Very odd. Very odd. Hard to believe," replied Nelson. He typed on his laptop. "How does a man who grows apples in the sticks in nowheresville get to liking crabmeat from a couple hundred miles away?"

"My wife grew up on the Eastern Shore. She got a teaching degree from the college in Salisbury and moved to West Virginia for a teaching job after graduating. We met, and we got married over thirty years ago."

"Is that right?" said Nelson with a smirk.

"There's not much crab anymore," said Knutson, shaking his head. "You can't get it in the supermarkets."

Nelson looked Roger over a moment, typed at his laptop a moment, and read something on the screen. He tapped his right thumb on his chin and asked, "Are you part of the black market in crabs, Mr. Lee? We know you stopped by a place called Blanton's that used to sell crabmeat years ago."

"How do you know I stopped by Blanton's?"

"We know. We know. You don't have to know why," answered Nelson. "It's not your business why we know. But we know."

"And I thought we lived in a free country."

Nelson snickered and said, "Even a free country needs security. Loosen up on security, and you might get less freedom. Terrorism and the like. Better security and the 9/11 bombing of the Twin Towers doesn't happen, and four planes don't get highjacked and slammed into buildings killing thousands of people. A totally free country leads to less security and less order. Don't you understand?"

"No."

"Well, you better get wise," said Knutson. "An absolutely free world is not consistent with security. Lack of security leads to dangerous conditions and even anarchy. We can't allow anarchy."

"So you can't have freedom in a totally free world," replied Roger, and he smiled shortly.

"What are you, Mr. Lee," Knutson shot back, "some sort of libertarian crazy? Some sort of counterculture radical? Another word for libertarian is anarchist." Knutson stepped toward Roger. "Your kind of thinking leads to a less secure country. Mr. Nelson and I work expressly to make our country more secure. It's our job. Our duty."

"Mr. Knutson and I have jobs to do. We are paid to make the country more secure," said Nelson.

Nelson strummed the table with his left hand and typed on the laptop with his right. He stared straight into Roger's eyes and asked, "So what is this Confederate bumper sticker on your truck?"

"I have ancestors who fought for the Confederacy."

"Your ancestors were traitors, Mr. Lee," said Nelson and Nelson grinned. Knutson and the security policeman chuckled.

"I don't think so. They were fighting for the land they worked and lived."

"Hmm," said Nelson. "They were fighting to keep slaves. Abraham Lincoln and his Union Army fought to free the slaves. Didn't you do your history lessons when you were in school?"

"My people had no slaves. Stonewall and the county had very few slaves. Almost none. If you knew anything about history, you would know that the people of the mountains had very few slaves."

Nelson chuckled and raised his left hand dismissively at Roger. "When we want a history lesson from a suspect, we'll ask you. But we don't want one at this time."

"Your problem, Mr. Lee, is that you have not kept up with the modern world," said Knutson. "To say that the Confederacy was evil is a given. That's taught in the schools by accredited teachers supervised by expert administrators. Jefferson Davis was evil because the expert administrators tell us so. Stonewall Jackson was evil for the same reason. Robert E. Lee too. All the men in gray. All evil. From the generals all the way down to the privates. Their statues needed to be demolished, and they were. Their posterity deserves to feel shame for their ancestors. The government in its wisdom wants you to be ashamed of your ancestors. Hate them. Hate them with passion." Knutson smiled broadly. "I am paid by that same government to make the country secure. I do as I'm told. The government is always right, at least as far as I'm concerned."

"The government owns you. Your heart and your soul," replied Roger. Knutson walked over to Roger and smacked Roger hard across the face. A small split opened over Roger's upper lip, and he could taste blood. A trickle of blood began to flow onto his lower lip, and Roger could feel wetness on his upper chin.

"Mr. Lee, we're government security police. We don't go by Miranda rights. We don't fool around. This is serious shit, not a debating club," said Nelson casually. "If you deserve violence, we can dish it out. Your Miranda rights were lost the moment you came into this room. Got it?"

"Right. But the government still owns you, and slapping me about can't take that away," said Roger, looking at Nelson.

Knutson rushed Roger and punched Roger with his right hand. Roger fell off his chair and to the left and lay sprawled near the table where Nelson sat. Another right hand sent Roger against the back wall of the room. The security policeman hit Roger across his right temple, and a burning sensation arose in his head. Roger rose as Knutson came at him. Roger hit at Knutson, but the punch was weak and did nothing to stop Knutson. Knutson pounded Roger back to the floor with a strong right, clipped Roger with a left hand, and landed a right hand to Roger's right eye and a cut began to flow blood. Roger tried to stand, but the security policeman hit him again, this time on Roger's right ear, and Knutson belted Roger with another powerful right hand, which further split the gash over Roger's right eye. Roger was now a helpless, bleeding clump on the floor. Roger kept his consciousness and looked up.

"If I were you, Mr. Lee," said Nelson with a chuckle, "I'd stay on the floor and wait for us to allow you to get back in your chair. You see, Mr. Knutson and I are professionals in this line of work. One of our jobs is to get uncooperative people like you to do what the government wants them to do. That's why it's called security. Mr. Lee, you're an unwanted throwback to a distant world. You aren't welcomed in this new world that the government plans for everyone who is respectful of the government and who obeys the government. If you are independent, you aren't worth much to the government. You make a living selling apples, huh? That's a shitty life if you ask me, but you don't need the government to survive. That makes you a dangerous person to the government. And as Mr. Knutson said moments ago, Mr. Knutson and I are paid by that government. You might say that you and independent people like you are a personal enemy of Mr. Knutson and myself."

Roger was bleeding heavily from the split above his right eye, and his right temple throbbed. He was stunned by the blows the two men inflicted, and he felt wobbly. Fire seemed to rage within his body, and he felt like vomiting. He could taste the scrapple he had eaten for lunch, thought he might throw it up, but he was able to suppress throwing up the scrapple. Hate flushed through Roger.

Roger was allowed to lie on the floor for a few minutes, and then Nelson said, "Mr. Lee, please sit back in your chair." Roger slowly rose, walked over to the chair, and sat.

"Very good, Mr. Lee," said Nelson. "I wish to conclude this interrogation. Mr. Knutson and I know that your sort of man hates people like us. You hate us, don't you."

"An hour ago I didn't even know you and Knutson. How did I hate you?"

"By being just who you are. An independent man who respects his ancestors. In your case, Confederate ancestors. The worst kind of ancestors."

"All the statues were torn down years ago. What do you want me to do, piss on the graves of my Confederate ancestors? My Confederate heroes?"

Knutson edged forward, pulled something metallic from his right pants' pocket, and slipped it onto his right hand. His face was menacing, and Knutson shot a full set of teeth. His eyes blazed hate.

"Your Confederate heroes are enemies of the state, and that makes them our enemies. Nearly two centuries in the past, and these dead men are still our enemies," said Nelson, and he waved his right hand dismissively. "They are only fit to despise, and those who wish to honor them are also fit to despise. You too, Mr. Lee. Your Confederate ancestors are deplorable. And you are deplorable." Nelson pointed at Roger with his right forefinger inches from Roger's face. Roger slapped the finger away, and Knutson was upon him, pounding him right and left until Roger was back on the floor with his two hands ineffectually trying to block Knutson's blows. Roger lost all consciousness.

Roger's limp body lay on the floor of the interrogation room. Nelson and Knutson smiled at each other. Both nodded their heads in affirmation. Nelson stood and pointed at Roger lying on the floor. "We better transport him to Arlington. Roger Lee is not important in the long run. But he's a security problem. Won't fall in line. Never will. Won't obey. Antigovernment. Counterculture. Has little respect for authority. He's a security risk, however insignificant he is as a person. Hell, he's just an apple farmer in the mountains, home to a bunch of inbred idiots with missing teeth and praying to Jesus and hunting and fishing and shooting off their guns and having sex with their sheep. He's an intolerable, that much is sure."

"It'll look good on our résumés that we captured such a disloyal subject," replied Knutson with a wide grin. "Should we have him transported tonight?"

"Yeah, I think so. I'll get us a secure van, and we'll transport that apple-farming son of a bitch to the HQ in Crystal City," said Nelson. "Lee ain't going anywhere on his own power for quite a while. He's one beat apple-farming son of a bitch." Nelson walked over to Roger and gave him a kick in the chest. Roger grunted, writhed a little bit, and then was very still. Knutson laughed.

"If he didn't like our questions, he certainly won't like what's in store for him in Arlington," said Knutson. "Yeah, the sad little bastard ain't going to like what's in store for him twenty-four hours from now. Independent old bastard. A dumb bastard too. They don't play games in Arlington. Questions are asked in Arlington, and the boys in Arlington don't like wrong answers." Both men guffawed.

Roger awoke in a very bright small room, and he was lying on a hard plastic bench. His head throbbed, and the stitches above his right eye provided shots of pain. He sat upright on the bench, and his stomach felt sour. He felt like throwing up, but he seemed to have little to throw up. He hadn't eaten in a long time, but he was not hungry. He didn't know how long he had been unconscious since Knutson and the security policeman had given him a beating. Pain pulsated at his left cheek, and he was sure that his cheekbone was fractured. He dimly remembered Knutson's brass knuckles pounding his face.

Roger was afraid of what might happen next. But he was also resigned to whatever fate was in store for him. He had no freedom of action. The government had taken that away from him. He wondered where he was. He had not been in this cell before. This was a different cell from the one he was jailed in on the Eastern Shore. Had he been transported? Was he even on the Eastern Shore?

A whimsical side of Roger was bemused by his quick fall. He was a totally free man only a few hours—or was it days?—ago. He had lost consciousness and had lost his sense of time since he was beaten. However many days ago it was, he just wanted to enjoy a road trip and enjoy a few beers and buy some crabmeat and go back to the mountains and eventually cook some of Connie's best crab recipes. Now he was wearing a red jail jumper in a security jail cell. That's right. When last conscious, he was wearing an orange jail jumper. So he must have been transported. And he had stitches over his right eye to close the wounds Knutson had provided. So he must have spent some time in a hospital or under the care of a doctor or nurse. But all that mattered was that Roger was a prisoner of the state for reasons unclear to him but had something to do with him being a free man who spoke his mind and told the truth as he saw it. But his political views—such as they were—were at variance of what the national government approved.

Sitting on the bench, Roger looked up at the wall before him. A small metallic device was attached to the front wall. A camera, of course. Being considered a criminal by the government meant surveillance. The government wanted the security apparatus to watch your every move. Perceived enemies of the state had no right to privacy.

Although he was afraid, Roger's boredom sitting there on the bench got the better of him. He thought he might as well say a Rosary. He crossed himself and decided to say the Glorious Mysteries. He began, "Our Father, Who art in Heaven, Hallowed be Thy Name. Thy Kingdom come, Thy will be done, on Earth as it is in Heaven, give us this day, our Holy Bread, and forgive us our trespasses as we forgive those who trespass against us, and lead us not into temptation but—"

"Quiet," demanded a loud, metallic male voice from the front wall. "Suspects are not allowed to talk in captivity unless spoken to. Suspects respond to questions that the government asks of the suspect and nothing more. Am I quite clear, Suspect Lee?" Roger did not respond.

Roger continued silently to say the rest of the Rosary he had started. Not only did it give him comfort and something to do other than stare at walls, he thought Jesus and Mary would appreciate him saying the Rosary under his current circumstances. He began to think about Franz Jagerstatter, a hero of the long past. What did Jagerstatter think when he was first arrested by the Nazis? He must have had the temptation to do as the Nazis wanted him to do and serve in the German army. Hitler's army. His village priest wanted him to serve. And so did his good wife, the mother of his three babies. Jagerstatter had a burden Roger did not have. Roger's wife was dead. His children were scattered throughout the country, so that his contact with them was tenuous. The people of the mountains with whom Roger lived did not know he was a captive of the state. What would they think when he was gone a week? A month? Roger wondered what his neighbors would do with his sheep and his chickens and his turkeys. The food and water he left his animals with must have run out by now.

Roger grew tired. He slumped over and collapsed onto the hard bench. His mind relaxed, and he did not dream. His brain was worn by stress, and his body was worn by the beating he had received. Roger slept on the bench for hours with no blanket in a room that was very cool. Security did not want Roger to be too comfortable. Roger was a threat to the government, so he deserved little comfort. The cold of the cell slowly began to wake him after his deep sleep, and he began to stir on the cold, hard bench. His mind began to work again. He soon felt a wave of dread, and his mind began to realize that his situation was dire and that his life could end at any time if the government wanted it to end. Roger did not see himself as a threat to the government, but the government had other ideas. And they had all the power.

Roger sat up on the bench. He was cold, and he rubbed his hands against his upper arms, but that did not make him any warmer. It was an instinct just like an animal's. He couldn't help wanting to be warm, but nothing he did could make him warm just sitting on the bench. So he rose and began to walk from the front wall to the back wall. He walked to the left wall and then to the right wall. He repeated himself. Front to back. Left to right.

A harsh feminine voice burst out, "Suspect Lee, you are ordered to sit down at once! Suspects are allowed to walk only when granted permission. And you are not given permission. Sit down on the bench, and keep your eyes forward. Do not speak. If you do not do as you are told, you will be punished severely. Do you understand, Suspect Lee?" Roger nodded his ascent and sat down on the bench.

He sat bored and frightened at the same time. So this was how totalitarians wore down their enemies? Roger, of course, had read of the communists and the Nazis and the fascists. But he never thought such tactics would be used on an insignificant and obscure apple farmer from the mountains like himself. Why was he important to the government? He was no threat. He had no power. He had no real political views. He was just a man happy to live on his own. Maybe that was why he was considered a threat. He lived independently as a man of the mountains. Just like Nelson said. Just being independent of the government made you an enemy of the government. Only the servile could be friends of the government.

The feminine voice from before announced, "Food is to be served momentarily. Sit perfectly still. An orderly will enter your room and lay a plate of food on the floor. You are not to move to eat it until the orderly has left and the door shuts. If you do not sit still, the food will be taken away. Do you understand, Suspect Lee?"

"Yes." Roger was famished. He hadn't eaten for what seemed to be two days. He sat obediently still as a heavyset, middle-aged Black woman in a gray uniform came into the room with a plastic plate of food and a plastic spoon. She spat in the food, sneered at Roger with contempt, sat the plate of food and the spoon on the floor, and left the room without saying a word.

"You may rise and retrieve your food, Suspect Lee," said the voice.

Roger stood and walked to the plate of food. The plate contained what looked to be half a can of Dinty Moore stew graced with the spit of the orderly and a slice of unbuttered Wonder Bread. No matter. Roger was hungry and would have eaten raw food just to eat some food and ease his hunger. He picked up the plate and spoon, walked back to the bench, and began to eat.

The feminine voice spoke as Roger finished wolfing down his small meal. "You are to place the plate and spoon on the floor before the door, Suspect Lee. When that is done, sit down on the bench perfectly still, so the plate and spoon can be retrieved, Suspect Lee? Do you understand, Suspect Lee?"

"Yes."

The Black female orderly opened the door five minutes after Roger sat on the bench. She carried a small container of what reminded him of the milk containers from his elementary school days. She placed the container on the floor, picked up the plate and spoon, turned toward Roger and said, "No mo' food till breakfast, old man." Then she left. Roger stood to pick up the container.

"No you don't," said the feminine voice. "You were not given permission to stand. Suspects are only allowed to walk or talk or eat when granted permission. You were not given permission to retrieve the container of milk. Suspect Lee, sit down at once. The orderly will retrieve your milk momentarily. By standing up without permission, you have forfeited your chance to nourish yourself. Let this be a reminder that all your actions at the present time are to be directed by the authorities of this institution. As a suspect, all your actions are to be sanctioned only by the permission of the Department of Security. All other actions independent of the Department of Security are to be proscribed. Do you understand the obedience you owe the legal authorities of the state and its guarantor, the Department of Interior Security, Suspect Lee?"

"Yes. I understand."

The container of milk was taken from the room a half hour later. Roger desired the milk. He was thirsty and hadn't had anything to drink since the beer he drank days before. But he obeyed. If he walked over to the milk container, he might be able to drink it before guards could stop him. But they would surely beat him for doing so. That was certainly implied by the feminine voice on the other side of the wall. The same orderly from before entered the room, grabbed the container of milk, and turned to Roger. "Bad luck, fool," she said, and she heartily laughed. She left the cell, and the door slammed shut behind her.

Roger sat for a while on the bench. His posterior became sore. For relief, he would slightly lift his left ham up off the hard bench for twenty seconds or so and then do the same thing with his right ham. Relief was short-lived, the pain alternating from one ham to the other.

"Suspect Lee, stop fidgeting," called out a voice from the wall. It was a Black female voice now.

Roger sat still a while and accepted the shooting pain in his buttocks. Why not stand? What could they do? Beat him? He already hurt badly. And then he noticed that his clothes were wet at the crotch. He must have urinated the last time he slept. He hadn't noticed. Roger began to realize that he was losing his humanity and his dignity by being confined by the authorities. He wet himself a few hours before, and now he sat in his own urine. He had eaten food that a prison guard had spat in and was happy to eat it. Perhaps *happy* wasn't the right word. Better said, his hunger was relieved to eat foul food. The authorities were breaking him, destroying him as a man.

Two hours went by. Roger slumped over, his elbows on his knees and his head between his knees. He slept. Confused dreams racked his mind. He was trying to fly away from the police with their nightsticks drawn, ready to beat him. He hovered above them for a few moments but slowly drifted back to the surface. The police came at him, and he propelled himself upward to safety. But then he descended once again back to the surface, losing his power of flight. The police came menacingly toward him once again, ready to pound him with their nightsticks. But again he was able to hover away just as the police were ready to beat him. Roger felt relief but wondered how long he would be able to evade the police. How long would he have the power of flight?

"Suspect Lee, stand," demanded the Black feminine voice that had spoken a few hours ago. Roger did not hear the voice and continued to be in a deep sleep. The demand was repeated very loudly, "Suspect Lee, stand. Stand up from the bench immediately. Or else you will be punished for insubordination." Roger's brain began to wake from his dreams. Peril and dread began to slowly sift into his mind. I must stand. I must stand. And Roger stood.

"Good," said the voice from the other side of the wall. "You are to bathe and exchange clothes. You have behaved dishonorably, Suspect Lee. You have soiled yourself. You smell badly. You are physically repellant to the staff of this institution. What do you have to say about your shameful behavior, Suspect Lee?"

"I am not ashamed. I don't want to be here. I only wanted to visit the Eastern Shore to buy some—"

"Silence!"

"Crabmeat."

"You must not talk, Suspect Lee. You are to be quiet. Be still. Stand completely still until your escort orders you to do more. Do you understand, Suspect Lee?"

"Yes."

Roger stood still, eighteen inches before the bench. Ten minutes went by. Were they ever to come? Of course they would, you fool. The authorities wanted him to wait in discomfort. The guards probably enjoyed toying with him. In authoritarian states, mean, nasty people flocked to the low-level positions. Almost every society that ever existed had mediocre men willing to use the whip on those they were instructed to whip. Or beat. Or execute. Spartacus and his followers were beaten and executed. The Barbary pirates and the Turks enjoyed whipping their Christian galley slaves, laughing at the sad men who sat in their own excrement while rowing the galleys that fought the Christian ships. These galley slaves had the further humiliation of their women being made sexual slaves for their Ottoman masters. And the Pole, Dzerzhinsky, created Lenin's secret police and was the heart of a killing regime that delighted in the murder of all possible threats to the regime, however insignificant. Hitler had his Gestapo, Mao had his Red Guards, and Pol Pot had the Khmer Rouge. Earth would always have ugly, vicious people.

The door of the cell opened. Two large, athletic Black men filed through the doorway followed by an equally large, older Black man. Each wore dark-blue uniforms with gold trim. Each had nightsticks on their left hips and sidearms on their right. All three had a name badge with their photos affixed to the left breast of their uniforms. The two younger guards wore sunglasses while the older guard did not. They walked toward Roger, their boots *clap-clapping* on the cement floor.

"You are to come with us, Suspect Lee," announced the older guard. The older guard turned and walked away toward the door, and Roger began to follow. The two younger guards walked behind Roger by about three feet, a guard on either side of him.

Roger and the three guards walked down the hall, went through doors to the left, walked down a short hall, stepped through another set of doors, and walked down a long hall. They passed other security in this hall, each wearing the same dark-blue uniforms with the gold trim. Most were Black or Latino. Many were women. Most wore sunglasses although they were deep inside a building. An attempt to intimidate? Perhaps. The four men reached a metal door, and the older guard placed a card against a square of computerized metal, and the door opened. The four men stepped inside.

"You are to disrobe. Take all your clothes off. You have pissed yourself. You may like wallowing in your own filth, but this is our place of work. You smell. You smell like an animal in a zoo. So get out of your clothes," ordered the older guard. The two younger guards impassively stared at Roger near the door.

Just then the Black female orderly who had spat in Roger's food and taken his milk entered the room. She was holding a large plastic bag. Behind her entered a white woman who looked to be in her midthirties. She wore a white medical lab coat that extended to her upper shins. Underneath, she wore black slacks. Her blond hair was chopped harshly at the nape of her neck. In her right hand, she held some sort of small notebook. She didn't speak and stood close to the door.

The orderly took five steps toward Roger and held open the large plastic bag with her two fattish hands. Roger said nothing and remained standing. The orderly then said with a sneer, "I don't plan on holding this bag open all day. Give me your clothes immediately."

"Off with your clothes. Get on with it," ordered the older guard. "Let's be quick about it."

"Is it normal for men to take their clothes off in front of women at this prison?" Roger asked.

"It is here. As a suspect, you have no privacy here. This orderly whose time you are wasting has seen hundreds of male suspects with their clothes off. It is part of the line of duty here," said the older guard.

"What is it you dislike about disrobing, Mr. Lee?" asked the female doctor from the front of the room. "That you are disrobing in front of two women, or that you are forced to disrobe in front of a woman of color?"

"No. Just that I'm forced to undress before two women. That's not a natural thing to do, at least where I live. I was brought up believing a man should be naked in front of one woman, his wife."

The female doctor gave a slight nod to the older guard. As if on cue, the older guard said loudly, "Take off your jumpsuit now!"

Roger unsnapped his jumpsuit and stepped out of it, catching his left leg on the crotch part of the uniform and lurched forward and onto the floor on his knees, part of his jumpsuit remaining on the lower part of his body. The orderly took two steps back, startled by Roger's tripping. Roger stood, took off the rest of the jumpsuit, limped to the orderly, and placed the jumpsuit in the extended bag.

"Slippers too," said the orderly. Roger pulled off his left slipper and then his right. He placed the slippers in the bag, and the orderly and the doctor left the room.

"Over here," said the older guard. He pointed to a small shower stall that did not have a shower curtain. Roger walked over to the shower stall. The two younger guards followed, and each took a position at each end of the stall. The older guard handed Roger an unopened bar of soap as he neared the shower stall. "You have two minutes to clean yourself," said the older guard. Then the older guard walked away from the shower to the center of the room.

The water in the shower was cold and shot out at half the usual intensity of a shower stream. The water never warmed and gave Roger no relief. Surely this was deliberate. The system that had complete control over him did not want him to experience anything close to relief or pleasure. He was to be kept in a regimen of stress and torment. He was to have no joy, however temporary or small. What were they after?

The orderly came back with a bag with a clean jumpsuit and slippers just as Roger finished his shower and stepped out. On a towel rack to his left was a towel. Roger's first instinct was to grab it, but he hesitated. Surely the towel on the rack was there for him to dry himself off with. And just as surely, Roger believed the guards would be angered by any independent action on his part.

"May I towel myself off?" Roger asked the guard to his left. The guard stared through Roger.

"How else are you going to get dry, fool?" said the orderly with contempt. So Roger toweled himself off.

The older guard walked toward Roger while the orderly turned her back and walked out of the room. The guard pointed at an unpartitioned toilet, about eight feet to the right of the shower. "Before you put on your clothes, you should relieve yourself right now while you have a chance. We don't like walking prisoners like you to the toilet all day. Takes up too much of our time. Do your business." The older guard walked away as Roger lifted the toilet seat and urinated.

Several hours later, Roger was sitting on the hard bench in his cell. He was increasingly disoriented about the time. Was it morning, afternoon, or evening? Roger couldn't guess. He hadn't seen sunlight for days. The artificial light had begun to depress him. He was dreadfully bored. Life in a prison was barren and dull. What kind of persons were attracted to prison work? Were they desperate for a job? Or were they drab, dull people who were content with their work? Maybe they found the regimentation of prison work something that made their lives relevant. Their lives were routinized, and they did not have to think for themselves. Superiors did their thinking. The guards were superior to the guarded, and that lifted their egos. It was edifying to know that you had a greater status than someone else, no matter how low those people were. And Roger was the lowest of the low now.

Roger was fed again. A new orderly, a chunky, middle-aged Latina, came into his cell with a bowl she placed on the floor. Without a word, she left. Under instructions, Roger walked over to the plastic bowl on the floor at the center of the room. It was a small bowl of tomato soup. A plastic spoon sat in the soup. Roger was happy for some sort of food. Roger had not had any food since the stew. He walked over to the bench and ate the soup in less than five minutes.

Less than an hour later, guards came for him. They were different guards than before. Two did not speak. One was Black, muscular, and very tall. The other was Hispanic and stocky, a little shorter than Roger. Both wore sunglasses. The lead guard was an albino Black man with freckles. He was husky and about fifty years of age. The albino flashed a short smile as if he knew what might be in store for Roger.

"Stand and follow me," said the albino. Roger complied, the two junior guards following slightly behind on each side of Roger. The four men walked down the hall but in the opposite direction of the shower. They went through a set of double doors into a large room. This room had a cluster of desks, some with monitoring devices. Two men, both Black, sat in chairs watching screens showing the many camera positions in the prison. They didn't even look up at the four as they passed. An older white man wearing black glasses sat at a smaller desk, typing furiously on a laptop. He looked up, distracted by the men, and then he was back at the laptop typing. Roger and the three guards stepped through another set of double doors and arrived at another hall. To the left of the double doors was an elevator. The albino guard placed a card against the security device and summoned the elevator. Thirty seconds later, they were riding upward. Roger noticed that the elevator stopped on the eighth floor. The doors of the elevator opened, and the four men got out.

The hallway that they entered was completely carpeted. It was beige and looked like the sturdy carpet found in a fine hotel at any exit off an interstate highway. Lights in glass sconces were spaced every thirty or so feet down the hall. This was a different world from the bleak world below the surface where Roger had spent his recent days. Similar to a hotel, doors were at forty-foot intervals down the hall. Each door had a white button and a small intercom outside the right of the door. The albino reached the fifth door on the left and pushed the white button. A buzzer sounded.

"Yes?" said a female voice.

"Sergeant Boykins. Suspect Lee is in my custody."

"Very good. We were expecting you. Please let Suspect Lee come in, Sergeant."

A mechanical latch sounded, and Boykins opened the door. Roger followed Boykins inside, and the two other guards followed.

At the far end of the room behind a solid oak desk was the same blond woman Roger had seen earlier in the day before he showered. Or was that yesterday? It didn't matter. Day and night did not matter. To her right was a man sitting in a plush mauve chair. He wore a white lab coat over a shirt and tie. He was in late middle age, stood a little over six feet tall, and was thin. The man had an angular face with an aquiline nose, and he was balding at his crown but had wiry gray hair around the rest of his head. His wire-framed eyeglasses were pushed up above his forehead. He could have been a college professor. To the woman's left was a short man with close-cropped dark brown hair. He looked to be in his middle thirties. This man was stocky, had a pug nose, and his face was dark and angry. He also wore a white lab coat. Behind the woman was a large window. Roger could see the Washington Monument in the far background. Was it still named after George Washington? Or was the name changed? No mind. A chair sat twenty feet before the woman's desk and faced her.

"Please sit down, Mr. Lee," the woman said amiably. She pointed to the chair. Roger walked over to the chair and sat. As Roger sat down, she said to the albino, "You may go, Sergeant Boykins." Boykins turned and left the room. The other two guards remained at the back of the room near the door. They knew the drill.

The woman looked at the laptop on her desk. She read for a moment, typed briefly, and smiled. "I see you've gotten in trouble with the security police. Something about buying crabmeat. Is that right?"

"Yes. I never thought buying crabmeat was a crime."

"Certain national delicacies are rationed by the national government. Crab is one. Lobster is another. Atlantic salmon is another. The government sees to it that there are enough of what are considered delicacies to go around with preference to certain areas of the country. For instance, the capital region receives a greater proportion of crab per capita than someplace like Kansas or Kentucky because the capital is not only considered more vital to the security of the nation, but also that the people of the capital can put crab to better use than a citizen living in the prairies or the mountains. You understand the concept, don't you?"

"That's interesting," said Roger. "And I was taught in college that the free market dictated the allocation of food. But I went to college a long time ago."

"That's an erroneous concept from the past, Mr. Lee. Swept away now," replied the woman. "Government intervention in the economy is absolutely vital, Mr. Lee."

"We are an urban nation now," interjected the younger man. He talked robotically and with contempt. "Many ideas from the past germinated in an agricultural society. That society is dead and gone even if there are some backward areas of the country that remain. Most of the precepts of the agricultural past have no relevance today. In fact, Mr. Lee, the residue of reactionary thinking that persists acts as a cancer in our modern, urban world." The older man nodded in assent and smiled.

"I am so discourteous, Mr. Lee. Let me introduce you to my two colleagues. To my right is Dr. Longchamp. He is a doctor of cultural anthropology." Dr. Longchamp nodded and made a sliver of a smile. "To my left is Dr. Yezhov. He is a doctor of political psychology." Dr. Yezhov made no acknowledgment to Roger but stared through him as if Roger was a bath towel or a piece of soap. "My name is Dr. Defarge. My doctorate was in feminist studies."

Dr. Defarge continued. "You are probably asking yourself why you are in a security prison."

"Yes. I didn't even know that security prisons existed before I was arrested. The concept never crossed my mind. When I was arrested, I wasn't exactly read my Miranda rights. I was told I had no Miranda rights. I've seen no lawyer. I've not been given a chance to call my family."

"Miranda rights do not exist for prisoners considered security threats," said Dr. Yezhov matter-of-factly. "Murderers have Miranda rights because they are not security threats. A murder in West Baltimore or Anacostia or South Chicago is of no consequence to the security apparatus of the nation. A bank robber receives Miranda rights because he or she is not a security threat. The bank robber is likely to have been born underprivileged or might also be of a minority group, so the crime might have been precipitated or induced by centuries of exploitation. Likewise, a shoplifter, a seller of fifty-dollar bags of marijuana or even a drunk driver. However, a man with reactionary views is a threat to the national security, and appropriate measures must be used to eliminate the security threat."

Dr. Longchamp spoke. "A man who advocates an absolutist position on the old Second Amendment, for instance, is a graver threat to the unity and security of our new, modern civilization we have been building than one hundred Chicago street criminals armed with assault rifles. The Chicago street criminal only kills his own kind and is not a threat to the security of the new civilization. He is cordoned off in the ghettos of the nation. But those who question authority in any way are threats, dire threats." Dr. Longchamp spoke as if enjoyed the sound of his voice. He was a self-important man.

It was Dr. Defarge's turn to speak. She smiled and said, "The greatest danger to the new world order is the independent man. A man who thinks for himself. A man with contrarian ideas. A man rooted in the discredited past. A man with reactionary ideas. People like that are not only beyond the pale, they are security risks."

"So I am thought to be a security risk? I am a simple apple grower with no political ambitions, who lives almost every moment of my life in the mountains," said Roger.

"It will be determined, in time, whether you are a security risk," said Dr. Defarge, and she tilted her head backward for a second and then leveled her head again. "That is why you are at the national security prison here in Arlington. You were not arrested for attempting to buy contraband crab. This tribunal is not concerned with your desire to acquire crabmeat. It is not our purview. But your attempt to purchase crabmeat that you are not allowed to purchase led to research on your intellectual life, Mr. Lee."

"Mr. Lee," said Dr. Yezhov. "What you do not know, and most Americans do not know, is that every person who is arrested or even pulled over for something as simple as a speeding ticket or running a red light is researched by the security research team two blocks from here. The computers they have are very powerful. The researchers are very thorough and very dedicated. For instance, if you write a letter to the editor of your local newspaper and express a view contrary to the interests of the security of the nation, it makes it to our security computers. The letter is reviewed and acted upon if the views expressed in the letter are deleterious to the security of the state. The same for any expression on the internet that is antithetical to the security of the state. Furthermore, if you make a reactionary statement at a restaurant or bar, a vigilant citizen could report it to authorities. It is easy for a vigilant citizen to report the reactionary or contrarian thoughts of other people. In fact, it is encouraged. Even the drunken thoughts of some uncouth slob at a bar can be investigated."

Dr. Yezhov chuckled and continued, "You might be surprised that many security risks have been uncovered by motorists being pulled over by some obscure deputy sheriff in some rural backwater. The deputy uses his computer to check on the motorist, and the information also comes here to Arlington, so we can check it. From Maine to Hawaii, from Alaska to Florida, all police activity comes under the scope of the security apparatus here in Arlington. Your average deputy sheriff or local cop does not even know that this is so. In addition, many security risks have bubbled up to the surface by simple automobile bumpers stickers that advocate views contrary to the security of the state. Some security risks have been discovered at a simple McDonald's or Red Lobster or even the beer line at a baseball game by patriotic citizens reporting people with reactionary views. People wearing T-shirts advocating reactionary views or values often have been reported and some have been arrested as security risks. You own a DVD of the old racist television series *All in the Family*, you are considered someone in sympathy with the reactionary views of Archie Bunker. You own a DVD of the reactionary actor John Wayne, you are a security risk. You own an old Washington Redskins football jersey, you are obviously a racist and are considered a security risk. Here in Arlington, information is king."

"You see, Mr. Lee," said Dr. Longchamp, "our security apparatus is the guarantor of our new order. Protection of our civilization demands the security apparatus." Dr. Longchamp placed his left hand on his chin, briefly sighed, and continued. "Our computerized society allows us to police security risks and examine them. Stalin, Hitler, and Mao never had this power to surveil their own people. The new state, with the power of the computer and the desire of the personnel of the state to use that power, makes us formidable. We know practically every aberrant political and social thought by any person living in this nation of over 350 million people. The modern state may not care with whom you may copulate with, but we do care to know what your private political or social views are. In any case, they aren't really private, are they?"

Dr. Defarge smiled. "So, Mr. Lee, you were brought to the attention of the national security apparatus when the security apparatus that defends crab supply at the Department of Agriculture's seafood division reported you to us in Arlington. But that was only seconds after the Department of Interior Security was already investigating you due to your truck bumper sticker. So the security state was alerted about you for two different reasons from two different government departments. You might call it overlapping bureaucratic security. While you were waiting in your car regarding some sort of traffic offense, your record was being run by the Department of Interior Security and the Department of Agriculture. The Department of Interior Security was concerned with your Confederate bumper sticker while the Department of Agriculture was concerned with your attempt to buy crabs. The Department of Interior Security was only seconds faster than the Department of Agriculture in realizing that you might be a security risk. So you were arrested and brought here. But both departments functioned well."

"I was knocked around and beaten and brought here," said Roger.

"The methods of security officers on the ground can be pretty rough. But it is a difficult, hard job," said Dr. Defarge. Dr. Defarge smiled insincerely and said, "I am sorry, Mr. Lee. I really am."

"How long have I been here? I've lost track of time."

"About four days," answered Dr. Defarge. "I am sure it was no holiday to be housed in the lower levels of the security department. The lower levels of this building aren't exactly filled with sensitive people. Even the national security apparatus has its dregs."

"Conditions were terrible," Roger said. "The food was scant and foul. I think it is that way to soften guys like me up."

"I won't dignify that with an answer," replied Dr. Defarge with a wave of her right hand. "This is not a holiday resort or a Hilton Hotel or a Cracker Barrel. This is a security installation."

"So I am here primarily due to the Confederate bumper sticker?"

"Yes. If your situation only involved the crabs, I think you would be out of here and back home. You might never had been arrested. But I am afraid there is a lot more about you, Mr. Lee," Dr. Defarge said slowly, deliberately, "that makes you a threat to national security." She looked down at her laptop. "Let's start with the Confederate flag. Why did you have a bumper sticker with a Confederate flag on it?"

"My ancestors fought in the Confederate Army. Also, I have a historic interest in the Civil War."

"You should have picked better ancestors, Mr. Lee," said Dr. Yezhov with a scowl on his face.

"They weren't mine to pick. And I am proud of them nonetheless."

"You know that your ancestors served on the wrong side of history," said Dr. Longchamp. He smiled weakly.

"They served on the losing side. Yes, they did. But I do honor their sacrifices."

"Sacrifice in a bad cause," Dr. Yezhov said with a nasty, angry tone. "Not only was the Confederate government one that supported slavery, it was also one that was opposed to the egalitarian aims of Abraham Lincoln." Dr. Yezhov bowed his head slightly.

"What egalitarian aims did Lincoln have? I didn't know he was a socialist. Lincoln might have done some bad things, but he was not a socialist. He was elected on the backs of Yankee industrialists."

"Let's not quibble, Mr. Lee. This is not a college debate we are conducting," said Dr. Defarge with a broad smile.

"But you do agree that the cause of the Confederacy was evil?" asked Dr. Yezhov.

"I stand with my ancestors. I stand with my people," Roger answered. "I am a man born in the twentieth century, so I naturally oppose slavery. My world is different than the world of 1860."

"The flag of the Confederacy stood in defense of segregation in the old South. It stood in defiance of the Civil Rights laws of the 1960s. Surely you don't support that flag?" asked Dr. Yezhov.

"Segregation ended long before my time. And we have very few Blacks in the mountains, so segregation was not a factor in our lives. Blount County had no plantations of any size. We had almost no slaves in Blount County. You can go weeks without seeing someone Black in Blount County."

"Are you pleased that Bland County—" said Dr. Yezhov.

"Blount. Blount County," Roger corrected.

"Yes. Blount County. Are you pleased that Blount County has so few African Americans today?"

"Not pleased or displeased. It is a fact that simply exists."

"What do you owe your ancestors, Mr. Lee?" asked Dr. Longchamp. He leaned back in his chair.

"Respect."

"Even when they were evil?" asked Dr. Yezhov.

"I don't consider them evil. They fought for the state of Virginia. They fought for their land. They fought for their people. They fought for their families."

"Your ancestors mean a lot to you, Mr. Lee," said Dr. Defarge.

"He's a real Shelby Foote type," cracked Dr. Yezhov.

"Yes. I defend my ancestors, as imperfect as they might have been. George Bernard Shaw, who was a socialist, once said that you must judge a man by the context of his times and not by the present time."

"What George Bernard Shaw said over a century ago is absolutely irrelevant," said Dr. Yezhov. "Nobody these days knows who this Shaw character was, and nobody cares that he ever existed. This Shaw you speak of is as relevant as an ant in the Sahara Desert." Dr. Yezhov switched gears. "For many, the Confederate flag is of the same equivalence as the Nazi flag. Are people correct to think that?"

"They can believe what they want. I don't consider the Confederate flag is in any way similar to the Nazi flag. I reject that idea entirely."

"Do you understand the term *deracination*, Mr. Lee?" asked Dr. Longchamp.

"Yes."

"What do you believe it means, Mr. Lee?" asked Dr. Longchamp.

"It means to uproot," Roger answered.

"Right," replied Dr. Longchamp. He paused and tapped his right hand on the arm of his chair. "In a cultural context, deracination is the cutting off of a modern person living now from his past. To make for a better, more equitable and peaceful society, our modern government has been implementing policies whose goals are to cut off people living today from any roots to the discredited past. The education system is the primary manner in which to deracinate people. Our government wants to deracinate its people while they are young. We hardly teach history in the modern schools, but when we do, we emphasize preferred people over the unpreferred. Harriet Tubman is emphasized over Robert E. Lee or Stonewall Jackson. Harriet Tubman is heroic. Lee and Jackson are villains. Reverend Al Sharpton is a guiding light, a spiritual savior of the nation. Billy Graham is religious trash, an anti-Semite, and friend of the contemptible Richard Nixon. As philosophers, Malcolm X is superior to Aristotle. Toni Morrison is taught in all the schools. Charles Dickens is rarely mentioned. Maya Angelou is considered a poet of greater importance than William Shakespeare. Maya Angleou is taught to all the children. Shakespeare is the poet for old fuddy-duddies like you and me. Hamlet and King Lear are confined to the few used bookstores that remain open. Othello is important due to other reasons that do not concern us at this tribunal."

"Soon they will be closed," interjected Dr. Yezhov. "Very soon." Dr. Yezhov smiled.

"Confederate statues and memorials were first to go for the obvious reasons," continued Dr. Longchamp. "They were easy to eliminate. And then Christopher Columbus. His voyages of exploration that opened America to white European exploitation was an inherent racist policy. White European exploitation not only killed off most of the Indians—"

"Indigenous population," Dr. Yezhov corrected.

"Of course. Indigenous population. The indigenous population was living in what for them was a paradise. But the whites killed off so much of the indigenous population that they decided to commit the ultimate racist act by making slaves of the Africans and forcing the African to do most of the work in the Americas under the gun of the white man. So Columbus was not only the root cause of the exploitation and disinheritance of the indigenous peoples, his voyages were also the root cause of the enslavement of the African. Columbus and the white Europeans who followed him were inherently evil, and we must be consider them evil in our eyes centuries later. And the indigenous peoples and the Africans were completely innocent victims of the white Europeans. So statues of Columbus were next to go. After Columbus, we have the American presidents to deal with. Any president complicit with any sort of exploitation were next to go. The slave presidents were easy. Washington. Jefferson. Madison. Jackson. Obscurities like Tyler who likely had few monuments. Nonslave presidents that defended slavery like Pierce and Fillmore had to go."

"But Millard Fillmore personally opposed slavery," said Roger.

"You know your history, Mr. Lee," said Dr. Longchamp with a smile. "Probably the last generation in this nation that knows anything about history. Notwithstanding Fillmore's personal views, he did sign the Fugitive Slave Law that came out of the Compromise of 1850. Very bad. Furthermore, Fillmore's 1856 presidential campaign running on the Know Nothing ticket puts him beyond the pale of decency. But Fillmore is as obscure as Tyler." Dr. Longchamp smiled. "I do think San Francisco renamed the Fillmore District a few years back when the citizens of that city realized how bad a man Fillmore was. I think they renamed it after some old ballplayer named McCarty—"

"McCovey," corrected Dr. Yezhov.

"Of course. McCovey. But that's beside the point." Dr. Longchamp leaned back in his chair and looked up at the ceiling and then looked back at Roger. "Racists of any type came next. Woodrow Wilson comes first to mind. Virtually all Southern politicians of the nation's first two hundred years had to be cleansed from the national memory. Ben Tillman all the way to William Fullbright. And then any person who essentially did little to nothing to fight for our modern concept of justice were deemphasized. Teddy Roosevelt. Dwight Eisenhower. The soldiers of the two world wars. Writers like Jack London, Ernest Hemingway and Willa Cather. Especially Mark Twain for his use of that ghastly word in *Huckleberry Finn*, of which I cannot say in public without bringing shame to this tribunal. Even Franklin Roosevelt, who acquiesced with the Jim Crow regimes during his presidency, had to go. A monument to him just across the Potomac had to be mothballed a few years ago, if memory serves. Eleanor Roosevelt, of course, is lauded as a lonely beacon of equality in dark times, and her name graces the obelisk across the river. So you get the idea, Mr. Lee. We of the modern state will wipe out the past as completely as possible. Only approved fragments will remain, historic figures like Eleanor Roosevelt who are useful to us."

Dr. Yezhov leaned forward in his chair, his dark eyes staring menacingly at Roger. Dr. Yezhov showed a mouth full of teeth. "Men like you are in the way, Mr. Lee."

"Doctors, we have more ground to cover," said Dr. Defarge, looking bored. "Let's move on."

Dr. Defarge once again looked onto her laptop, read for a moment, and asked Roger, "You have pretty absolute positions of the Second Amendment. Is that correct?"

"Yes. I believe the Second Amendment gives Americans the right to bear arms."

Dr. Defarge rolled her eyes and smiled. "You have maintained an extremist position on the Second Amendment for quite a long time. Our information provided to us by the security research division says that you have written two letters to the editors advocating the extreme position on the Second Amendment. One letter way back in 2011. Another more recently in 2023. And there's dozens of comments you've made on the internet supporting the extreme position on the Second Amendment. Quite a record."

"Do you think the Second Amendment allows a private citizen to own a machine gun or a tank?" asked Dr. Yezhov.

"The Second Amendment was written before either the tank or the machine gun existed," Roger answered. "The spirit of the Second Amendment would seem to allow private individuals to own any weapon to defend his liberties."

"A nuclear bomb?" asked Dr. Yezhov. "Would you allow a private citizen to own his or her own nuclear bomb?"

"What the Second Amendment implies is that a citizen can own any weapon for his defense of his liberties. The world has changed a lot since 1787, that's for sure. The world of Daniel Boone no longer exists. I do grant that private individuals should not be allowed to own nuclear weapons, tanks or rocket launchers. Not so sure about machine guns. They can be broadly defined to include firearms that aren't true machine guns. So I might be described as not ideologically pure on the Second Amendment. Or what used to be the Second Amendment."

"Do you hunt?" asked Dr. Yezhov.

"Yes," Roger replied.

"Why do you hunt? The grocery stores are filled with meat," said Dr. Defarge.

"I like the taste of venison. And I do enjoy hunting. Hunting and fishing are sports we like best in the mountains," answered Roger.

"Why?" asked Dr. Defarge. She wore a puzzled look on her face.

"Hunting is a skill. A deer just doesn't walk up to a hunter and allow it to be shot. A hunter must outthink a deer to be in a position to shoot it."

"Outthinking a deer doesn't seem to be a very difficult thing to do," said Dr. Yezhov.

"Unless you are actually trying to do so," Roger replied. "It is a little harder than you would think."

"Do you agree that handguns are not needed to hunt?" asked Dr. Yezhov.

"No. Most hunters prefer shotguns or rifles or crossbows to hunt. But I've known hunters to use handguns to hunt. But that's not the point of the old Second Amendment. The old Second Amendment didn't guarantee the right to hunt. It used to guarantee the right to bear arms."

"Why would you want a handgun?" asked Dr. Yezhov.

"Self-defense," answered Roger. "And to shoot targets. They are enjoyable in themselves."

"But they are illegal to own," snapped Dr. Yezhov.

"Do you think the owners of handguns just handed over their handguns just because the government told them to? Nobody I know complied with the law that was passed making handguns illegal."

"So you advocate the breaking of the law, Mr. Lee" asked Dr. Yezhov.

"I would rather think I am ignoring an unjust law and not that I am breaking the law. The old Second Amendment guarantees the right to keep and bear arms. Pretty simple English. So I do believe in the old spirit of the Second Amendment. Yes, I do."

Dr. Longchamp looked thoughtfully at Roger. He leaned back in his chair and slid his forefinger against his chin. He sat up straight and asked, "Mr. Lee, do you think the right to bear arms permits an individual or a group of individuals to proclaim a rebellion or insurrection against the government?"

"I do. Even Thomas Jefferson thought that a little rebellion now and then was a good thing. The American Revolution was a successful rebellion against the authority of King George."

"Thomas Jefferson was a fool. And even he had an insurrection act passed late in his presidency," said Dr. Yezhov. Dr. Yezhov looked hard at Roger, his eyes black marbles of hate. "Mr. Lee, do you advocate rebellion against the duly elected authorities of the nation?"

"I am a simple apple farmer in the mountains of West Virginia. I don't advocate nor support rebellion. Even if I did, nobody would listen. I am of no consequence to the world outside my mountain community. I just want to be left alone."

"It is difficult for the authorities to ignore your radical views," said Dr. Defarge.

"They weren't always radical views," Roger answered.

"Times change, Mr. Lee. Perhaps you should change with them," said Dr. Yezhov.

Dr. Longchamp sat forward in his chair, his hands on his knees, and said, "A civilization grows organically and aspires to higher ideals once it becomes confident in itself. Higher ideals like equality become a guiding light and a beacon of progress. Women become the equals of men. African Americans become the equals of white Americans. The LBGQTIP community becomes the equals of heterosexuals. As this process occurs, primitive, discredited ideas are swept away. The private right to own weaponry is abandoned. The right to rebel against the current beneficent regime is forbidden. Churches are forced to provide wedding services to same-sex couples or lose their tax-exempt status even if same-sex marriage violates their centuries-old beliefs. In agriculture policy, the growers of arugula, brussels sprouts, and all fruits are subsidized and cattle ranchers are penalized. Inevitably, because of their superior virtue, obedience to the elite is rewarded. In that way, civilization marches forward."

"You want to go forward, Mr. Lee. Don't you?" asked Dr. Yezhov.

"I won't abandon my principles to get along."

Dr. Defarge shook her head and smiled. "You are a stubborn man, Mr. Lee."

"Stubborn man or not, Mr. Lee, your views present a security risk to the legal authorities of the state," said Dr. Yezhov. Dr. Yezhov looked over at Dr. Defarge and said, "Teri, I think we have enough on Mr. Lee to present a very strong case against him as a security threat. I would believe the upper echelon of the security on the third floor would agree."

"Is this being taped?" Roger asked.

"Of course," answered Dr. Yezhov. "All interrogations are taped. And they are viewed by security agents as the interrogations are conducted and reviewed afterward if the situation warrants review."

Dr. Defarge looked over at Dr. Yezhov and said, "Doctor, I have a little more territory to explore regarding Mr. Lee." She looked at her laptop and then looked over at Roger. "Mr. Lee, from your Internet posts, you seem to have an archaic idea regarding the size of the government. Very restrictive views on the proper size of government. That is regarded as an outmoded concept that doesn't fit with our enlightened age. We now know in our progressive age that big, responsive, ubiquitous government is required to provide succor to our citizens. Why don't you agree?"

"Because I believe it is very important to be independent and free," answered Roger.

"That's an arrogant thing to say," said Dr. Yezhov. "And self-delusional. We are interdependent citizens. No man should or can be completely free."

"Completely free, no. I am not a libertarian purist. I am rooted in my community and obey the laws and live by the customs of my community. But I like to think of myself as relatively independent and free," said Roger.

Dr. Longchamp spoke. "Modern government frees us from the barbarism of the past, Mr. Lee. Modern government provides so many things people want. A woman with no husband and three children who aren't supported by a man are given food, an apartment, and child care by the government. That is the civilized thing to do. An intelligent young woman wants to become an artist. The government pays for her college tuition, and her room and board. That is the civilized thing to do. A young man wants to become a doctor or a lawyer or a chef or a geologist. The government pays his way. That is the civilized thing to do. A man wants to become a woman. The government pays for the operation and the various treatments. That is the civilized thing to do. A museum needs funds to acquire paintings and to run its operations. The government pays for that. A generous government is a civilized government."

"How about self-reliance? How about making your own way? Man needs to be free to succeed or fail. A man needs self-respect," said Roger.

"That is the old thinking," replied Dr. Longchamp with a slight smile. "It went out when industrial capitalism forced us to alleviate the pains and agonies created by that system and forced the enactment of the welfare state. You support the welfare state, Mr. Lee?"

"Yes. To a degree. But I don't think the welfare state should coddle people."

"In any event, the days of laissez-faire and total freedom had to be vanquished by a new social structure where the government is paternalistic toward its citizens. The new system was to ameliorate the ruthlessness of industrial capitalism. Andrew Carnegie, John D. Rockefeller, Henry Ford, and even an archaic figure like Daniel Boone lost out. Civilization won. And the modern businessman realizes that government intervention in the economy is superior to laissez-faire. It can't be denied that our modern government provides more social cohesion and harmony than the old brutal way of the old past with a hands-off government. The modern businessman works with the government gladly and supinely. The modern businessman makes his money, sure, but in a way that the government approves." Dr. Longchamp paused and raised his right forefinger. "An altruistic government is key. The old concept of small government is absurd. It makes as much sense as Divine Rights of Kings. The concept of small government as a good in itself as opposed to a magnanimous, ubiquitous, and humanitarian government that we have today is like comparing a primitive outhouse with modern toiletry. Mr. Lee, you are surely out of date if you support the concept of small government."

"Small government is as relevant as using leeches to bleed patients," growled Dr. Yezhov.

Dr. Defarge once again looked at her laptop. She ran her left hand through her blond hair, pushing it back away from her forehead. She tapped her keyboard and read some more.

"Immigration appears to be an important issue for you. It would appear by our research that you commented on immigration at least one hundred times on the Internet," said Dr. Defarge.

"Closer to two hundred times, Teri," interrupted Dr. Yezhov.

"Why is immigration an important issue for you, Mr. Lee?" asked Dr. Defarge.

"Immigration changes a nation," Roger replied.

"But we are a nation of immigrants," said Dr. Yezhov.

"That's a simple truism," said Roger. "America is different than it was five hundred years ago because of European immigration. European immigration radically altered America's demographics. The America of today is radically altered from the America I was born fifty-eight years ago. The United States will soon have a Third World majority. Yet the United States was 80 percent white when I was born. That is a radical change."

"So you are a racist, Mr. Lee?" asked Dr. Yezhov, his teeth baring like fangs and his tone angry.

"That's what you are saying. I'm not saying it. *Racist* is a term that gets thrown around a lot, so much that most people don't even understand the term. It is sort of a blanket insult used to shut people up. I don't consider myself a hater. Hate is a waste of emotion."

"How can we think of you otherwise, Mr. Lee, when you say the nation is undergoing radical demographic change," said Dr. Defarge.

"Is it not true?"

"What is true?" asked Dr. Defarge.

"That our country is undergoing radical demographic change. It has certainly been a radical demographic change. And the majority of Americans haven't been asked why the change was necessary."

"What the average person thinks regarding the complicated issue of immigration is unimportant. Well-educated elites, schooled at the finest universities, are better able to deal with such a complex issue as immigration," said Dr. Longchamp. He rose a bit in his chair. "We elites have a better grasp of the issue of immigration than your average American. For instance, there is an economic side to the dilemma of immigration. Can immigrants be a net positive for the economy? Do they perform jobs that other Americans will no longer do? Can they keep the price of labor down, which allows for cheaper prices and increased profits? Do they do vital jobs like performing as nannies or housekeepers so that educated women can work outside the home instead of wasting their minds doing mundane, tedious, and joyless work running households? Do these immigrants vote for the political aims of the nation's elite when they are granted the vote?"

"So the immigrants vote for the right party and keep the wages of working-class Americans down, correct," said Roger.

"That's a very simplistic way of putting it, Mr. Lee," replied Dr. Longchamp with a smile.

"It doesn't matter what you think about immigration, Mr. Lee," said Dr. Yezhov with a sneer. "It doesn't matter what any of your kind thinks about immigration. We want it to happen, so it is going to happen." Dr. Yezhov sat forward in his chair and grinned.

"It will be better that America has no ethnic or racial core. America will become a multicultural nation and will be a proud model for the world," said Dr. Longchamp.

"Even that idiot from Texas, Dubya, agreed," chimed Dr. Yezhov.

Dr. Longchamp continued. "A century from now, I can see a Europe where no nation has an ethnic core or a racial core. The nations will be only organizational bodies for a wise, altruistic government that provides for all. I would like to see Germany with as many ethnic Turks as ethnic Germans. I would like to see France with as many Algerians, Moroccans, and Africans as Frenchmen. I would like to see a Sweden with as many Arabs as Swedes. I would like to see an England with as many Muslims as Englishmen. I would like to see an Italy with as many north Africans as Italians."

"Of course, interethnic breeding will be encouraged and promoted," said Dr. Defarge. "In fact, I find it a very hopeful sign when I see so many mixed marriages in the capital's suburbs. I especially like it that so many white females are attached to African American men." Dr. Defarge smiled broadly. "You don't like that, Mr. Lee?"

"The romantic lives of others do not concern me," Roger answered.

"But do you like to see interracial couples?" Dr. Yezhov asked.

"It is not my business. But I don't really care to see it, honestly. You don't see it often in the mountains."

"Your honesty is to be commended even if it will be held against you," replied Dr. Yezhov.

"Mr. Lee," said Dr. Defarge. "Do you realize your response was the response of a primitive person? It is backward and reactionary."

"It was what I expected," said Dr. Longchamp, and he nodded at Dr. Yezhov. "Very skillfully played, Doctor. We have Mr. Lee pinned as a racist." Dr. Longchamp chuckled briefly. "Reactionaries cling to the past. Their love of guns. Their love of absolute freedom. Their love of ethnic solidarity. Their love of racial purity. They have no real future."

There was a pause. Dr. Defarge looked to her right at Dr. Longchamp, and he nodded. She looked to her left, and Dr. Yezhov sat impassively but said nothing. "Let's move on," she said, and she looked at her laptop and read for a moment.

"Mr. Lee, you seem to have a hostility toward the LBGQTIP community. Is that true?" asked Dr. Defarge.

"I don't hate anyone. I have no hostility toward homosexuals," Roger answered.

"But you don't support gay marriage," said Dr. Yezhov. "That's a clear sign that you hate the LBGQTIP community."

"I don't agree," replied Roger. "Ancient Rome and ancient Greece tolerated homosexuality to a great degree, but they never conferred the rite of marriage on homosexuals. The idea of homosexual marriage is new. Nobody conceived of it before recent times. No president until this century ever supported homosexual marriage. Not Franklin Roosevelt. Not Lyndon Johnson. Not Bill Clinton, at least as president. Nobody. If either John F. Kennedy or Richard Nixon had come out in support of homosexual marriage in the Kennedy-Nixon debates of 1960, they would have been considered insane and would have been asked by party leaders to step down as the candidate."

"That's ancient history," said Dr. Yezhov. "From an unenlightened era dead and buried."

"You are locked into the past, Mr. Lee," said Dr. Longchamp. "That is very dangerous. People who don't get on board with progress get left behind. There is a brand-new world out there that we have been constructing for decades now. Those with static values will be trampled by the inevitable changes."

"What if tens of millions don't want to change their values?" asked Roger.

"They will change whether they like the changes or not. Or they will accept them and keep their mouths shut. These changes are inevitable," said Dr. Yezhov. "You can't hide from the system. Sure, you can isolate to a degree in some unimportant and irrelevant mountaintop or a valley. But the system will control you whenever it wants to. Even in the mountains, we run the schools. We shape the children. What the government doesn't shape the children through the schools, our cultural dominance shapes the children through Hollywood and television and the music industry and the Internet. Each is an ally of the government. We are really quite powerful. People who think like you are very weak."

"So you don't support gay marriage?" asked Dr. Defarge.

"No."

"You don't support sexual equality?" asked Dr. Defarge.

"No."

"Do you think two men can fall in love and want to be married? Do you think two women can fall in love and want to be married?" asked Dr. Defarge.

"Yes. They may want to be married but wanting it doesn't make it so."

"You are so stubborn. Everyone under the age of fifty believes in gay marriage. Even most churches have come on board," said Dr. Defarge.

"And the ones not on board are rightfully penalized," shot Dr. Yezhov. "Churches not on board with gay marriage will be hounded and inevitably change or be rubbed out."

Dr. Defarge frowned, and her face seemed to narrow. Her eyes became dark brown pellets as she viewed her laptop. She turned from the laptop, placed both elbows on the desk, and lowered her face to her arms and looked back up.

"Mr. Lee, you seem to have reactionary views on the equality of the sexes. Is that true?" asked Dr. Defarge.

"I don't see that my views are reactionary. I view that men and women are different. They have different bodies. They tend to have different roles in society."

"But that's sexist," replied Dr. Defarge.

"Neanderthal thinking, Teri," sniped Dr. Yezhov.

"Of course," said Dr, Defarge, turning her face shortly to Dr. Yezhov. She looked annoyed. Was she angry that Dr. Yezhov called her by her first name? Dr. Defarge turned back to Roger. "You do believe in equality of the sexes, right?"

"Equality in importance, yes. I had a wife who died a few months ago. I have two daughters. I cherish and love each as I love my two sons. My wife and two daughters are different from my two sons because each has given birth to children while my sons cannot biologically give birth. That is one of the ways that make them different. Both my sons played football in high school while my daughters did not."

"Why is that so?" asked Dr. Defarge. "Don't you think women could play football along with the boys?"

"That's silly," said Roger, and he grinned. "Boys have different bodies than girls. Boys are bigger, stronger, and faster. Boys have much more testosterone than girls. It has been a long time since my school days, but I think I remember that males have twenty times the testosterone than females. That's a big difference."

"That can be remedied," said Dr. Yezhov.

"Why would mankind want that? I enjoy the differences between men and women," said Roger.

Dr. Defarge smiled. "Very quaint, Mr. Lee. But much out of date. You like the old sex differences because men have dominated women throughout history. But we have evolved from the old patriarchy, at least most of us. Complete equality is the goal."

"But men will never have babies," Roger shot back.

"That is insignificant, Mr. Lee," said Dr. Yezhov. "And modern science is working on ways to change that fact."

"I think I'll be long dead before men start having babies," said Roger.

"Why don't you believe in complete equality of the sexes?" asked Dr. Defarge.

"Because men and women are so biologically different. Men and women are emotionally different as well," answered Roger.

"How so, Mr. Lee?" asked Dr. Defarge.

"Women are far more nurturing. Men have harder hearts."

"That's a generalization, Mr. Lee. I know men who are very nurturing and women with hard hearts," said Dr. Defarge.

"Yes. I agree. But that's not the norm. There aren't many Lady MacBeths out there," responded Roger.

"Do you think women today are liberated from the old patriarchy?" asked Dr. Longchamp.

"Perhaps in ways. But the old patriarchy didn't have a 50 percent illegitimacy rate. It didn't drive mothers out of the home, leave her kids in day care, and work for a living," said Roger.

"Most women, with children or not, prefer working a career rather than changing diapers and mopping the floor or making sure dinner is on the stove when her husband gets home," said Dr. Defarge.

"So you believe in patriarchy, Mr. Lee?" asked Dr. Yezhov.

"Many aspects of it. Yes. I believe in families. I believe in marriage. I believe in husbands and wives. I believe in fathers and mothers."

"Don't you think that the old patriarchy held back women?" asked Dr. Defarge.

"In some ways. Perhaps. But most work is not fun. Most work can be a grind. Working within the home might be more rewarding for women than working outside the home."

"Do you think men should dominate society?" asked Dr. Defarge.

"Men have always dominated societies throughout the history of the world because men are stronger and more ruthless. Men make better warriors, and most societies in the past were based on the accomplishments on the battlefield and the accomplishments behind the plow," said Roger. "Think of all the inventions that have made life easier and have made societies much more economically productive. Almost all those inventions, especially in the past five hundred years, have been invented by men and white men at that." Roger could see Dr. Yezhov flush red while Dr. Defarge shook her head slowly.

Dr. Defarge looked hard at Roger, chuckled softly, and said, "Congratulations, Mr. Lee. You reveal yourself to be a sexist and a racist in the same sentence."

"I didn't mean to. I was just trying to state a fact."

"But the only reason men have made most inventions is that men have subordinated women for centuries," said Dr. Defarge.

"Maybe men subordinated women because they had the power to do so," said Roger. He knew it was a stupid remark the moment he made it.

"And that makes it right?" snapped Dr. Defarge, her voice shrill.

"It makes it so. I did not say it makes it right."

"Shouldn't the government make it right?" asked Dr. Defarge.

"I don't see why or even how the government should intervene in the relations of men and women. How can the government micromanage the private affairs of men and women in a nation of 350 million people? Is it even possible?"

"Be assured, Mr. Lee, that the government is quite capable in intervening into any field of human conduct that is worth the effort," said Dr. Yezhov. "The conduct of some drug addict in the hills of Kentucky is not worth the government wasting time on even if he beats his girlfriend and neglects his children. They are trash. But the government wants to direct the behavior of people who are vital to society. A man with sexist thoughts who has economic power or political power must be subordinated to the public good and must be made to accept female equality and be happy to do so. So if a man runs a company of five hundred employees, and his company has four vice president positions, half should be female. Half the employees should be women. Half the vice presidents should be women."

Roger interrupted, "And if the company is one that harvests trees for lumber, or fishes the Bering Sea in Alaska, or is in construction, occupations that are about 99 percent male, they should be made half female by government decree?"

Dr. Yezhov waved his left hand and laughed. "Those are muscle professions. Not important."

"Not important," responded Roger with a chuckle. "How would we have houses to live in without the work of lumberjacks, woodworkers, and construction workers to build the houses. Or men who go out to sea and fish for the seafood we eat. It is almost all men who do those sorts of jobs. I'd say that those men do pretty important work."

Dr. Yezhov shook his head. "Mr. Lee, you are a troglodyte. We are entering a new world. The diversity trainer is more important than the carpenter. The personnel manager is more important than the lumberjack. The company psychologist is more important than the deep-sea fisherman. The computer technician policing the Internet is more important than the construction worker. The lowest clerk in the Department of Agriculture is more important than the individual farmer. Get your head on straight, Mr. Lee. The cognitive elite is more important to the modern state and the society we are forming than those people who do the actual physical labor."

"So you mean that people who actually produce something of value that consumers need or want are lower than the cognitive elite you speak of?" asked Roger.

Dr. Yezhov replied, "Every society has an elite that determines distribution of wealth. We of the government elite get a major portion of the wealth today, and the laborers get the crumbs. So it has always been whether it is medieval Europe, nineteenth-century Britain, ancient China, the Roman Empire, or America in the era of the robber barons. John D. Rockefeller didn't make the oil, but he controlled it and became rich controlling it. His workers got to live in shacks and worked seventy-two hour weeks and ate corned beef and cabbage. Rockefeller's children lived like kings eating lobsters and steaks and were taught by tutors and lived in fifty-room houses."

Dr. Defarge raised her right hand and softly slapped it at a for- ty-five-degree angle toward her desk but short of her laptop. "This is not a college debating class. Mr. Lee, we are not here to debate you. We are here to explore your views, most of which seem reactionary and are unworthy of respect."

Dr. Defarge tapped at her laptop a moment. Roger looked to his left and saw that Dr. Longchamp looked bored and seemed close to dozing off. Dr. Yezhov glared. "One last item before we conclude, Mr. Lee. You have a great interest in Western civilization. Why is that?"

"Because I was born a child of Western civilization," Roger replied.

"Why leave out other civilizations?" asked Dr. Defarge.

"Because I am part of Western civilization."

"Do you have no respect for other civilizations?" Dr. Defarge asked.

"Yes. I have great respect for many civilizations. The Chinese in particular. But I am not Chinese and am not a child of Chinese civilization."

"What do you consider Western civilization?" asked Dr. Longchamp.

"Shakespeare. Dickens. Galileo. Newton. Da Vinci. Dostoyevsky. Plato. Aristotle. Beethoven. Frank Sinatra. Baseball. The Bill of Rights. Guarantees of personal freedom. Government by consent. The many machines that make lives easier and more reward- ing. Christianity," answered Roger.

"Those are all old men that you mentioned," said Dr. Yezhov. "Dead white men. They are men of the very old past. As for the concepts that you mentioned, the idea of government by consent is only nominal. Our new system controls the levers of power, so we control the people, usually indirectly so that the people do not know that the government is controlling them. We control the information the people receive. We can even control the vote totals if needed but this is rarely needed. As for the Bill of Rights, it is an archaic relic of the late eighteenth century that is about as relevant as the Roman Senate was during the Roman Empire. As for Christianity, it exists only in pockets of rural America. It has all the relevance of an Elks Lodge or a barbershop quartet of old. Very few young people care for it. Christianity is scorned in the schools, so the children get the drift. They learn that only losers are Christians."

"Christianity will always exist as long as Christ exists. And He will always exist," replied Roger.

"That's happy talk, Mr. Lee," said Dr. Yezhov with a smirk. "Christ is like an aged singer who plays to small, dwindling crowds of senior citizens. The curtain is coming down on Christ and Christianity, I am afraid, Mr. Lee."

"There will always be a remnant. If it leads to martyrdom, so be it," said Roger.

"Do you want to be a martyr, Mr. Lee?" asked Dr. Defarge.

"No. Not really. I am not so brave as that. I just want to live out my days in my mountains, near my river, and on my farm."

"Life is not so easy," said Dr. Defarge. "You have been designated a security risk. We here are attempting to determine how grave a risk you are." She turned to Dr. Longchamp and then to Dr. Yezhov. "But I think we are finished with you today. We've covered a lot of ground, and a lot of it is not edifying."

Dr. Defarge pushed a button at the side of her desk and whispered into it. After speaking, she sat bolt upright in her chair and said, "Mr. Lee, you will be confined down the hall. You will find it more comfortable than the cell you were detained these past few days. We don't believe in degrading and brutalizing our prisoners up here on the eighth floor. Your food and drink will be adequate, and there is a small bed for you to sleep on." Her eyes looked past Roger and at the two men at the back of the room. "Guards, please transport Mr. Lee to Room 828."

Roger had barely remembered that the two guards had never left the room during the interrogation. The two men stood and walked over to where Roger sat. Roger instinctively stood. The shorter of the two guards motioned Roger forward, and Roger obediently walked to the door.

Room 828 was carpeted in deep burgundy and was the size of a room in a cut-rate motel on a rural interstate. A crisply made queen-sized bed lay halfway into the room and to the right perpendicular to the door. A small table and a chair sat to the left near the front door. To the rear of the room was a bathroom with a bathtub, shower, and sink. White towels sat folded on plastic racks. Two small bars of wrapped soap sat at the right hand of the sink. It could have passed for a room at a Super 8 but for the fact that there was no television, chest of drawers, or small refrigerator.

"Dinner will be served in half an hour," the smaller guard said dully. The two guards left the room, the door shutting with a loud metallic clacking noise. Roger was locked in. He didn't even bother to try to open the door.

Nothing to read or watch but knowing that food was half an hour away, Roger decided to shower. He stripped out of his prison clothes, turned the shower on to the hottest possible setting, moderated the knob so he wouldn't scald, and stepped into the shower. The hot water soothed Roger. Although it was a long while since he was beaten by the security officers on the Eastern Shore of Maryland, he was weary from the stress of prison life and the questioning of the three doctors. The shower was luxury, and he almost felt delirious. For a very brief moment he was not some criminal designated by the state but a man with muscles, blood, a heart, two lungs, and a brain. But Roger's content was short-lived. The brain told him that the shower was an ephemeral respite. The security apparatus would be at him again.

Roger damned himself for his honesty with the three doctors. He should have said as little as possible and passed himself off as an ignorant yokel from the mountains. He was stupid to be honest. Very stupid. The doctors did not like his answers. That was why the questioning took so long. If he had been just a coward or a dolt, he might be off the hook and heading home. Sure, the doctors had access to everything Roger had said in the various media, and there were many things he had written that would strike the government as repugnant. But much of what he had written was in the long past, and he could have explained that he had progressed in his thinking. But what he said to Dr. Yezhov, Dr. Defarge, and Dr. Longchamp was fresh and current like an open sore. Damned stupid.

Roger feared Dr. Longchamp the least. He seemed to be an arrogant, self-absorbed, high-browse sort of academic happiest in his study with several bookshelves filled with books lined along the walls and a mahogany desk and a comfortable arm chair where he wrote long essays that were intended for fellow academics like himself. He didn't seem to be capable of being mean. Dr. Longchamp seemed to be bored by the proceedings.

Dr. Yezhov was mean and very hostile. Roger knew that Dr. Yezhov hated him personally. Dr. Yezhov would gladly order a firing squad to shoot him dead like Czar Nicholas or have him hanged like Tuco in a Western film he had seen as a teen. Yes. *The Good, the Bad, and the Ugly.* They didn't play that on the television any longer. Westerns were viewed as socially reactionary by the government and weren't played on television any longer except for a few newer Westerns where the white man was portrayed as evil. No matter. People still had DVDs for now, but DVD players were hard to buy these days, and eventually DVDs would become obsolete. John Wayne and Clint Eastwood would vanish down the memory hole eventually. People like Dr. Yezhov would make it so.

Dr. Defarge was hard to figure. She did little questioning, didn't show much emotion, and let Dr. Yezhov do most of the actual interrogating. She almost acted surprised when she looked at her laptop and documented Roger's reactionary views. She seemed cold and dispassionate, closer in personality to Dr. Longchamp without his sense of self-importance. She was younger than her two colleagues, which probably meant that she was better indoctrinated in the modern values that the government had been trying to instill in the schools for decades. That chopped hair was a clue to her personality. A feminist hairstyle, for sure. She was probably as mean as Dr. Yezhov but hid her emotions more effectively.

Roger finished the shower, dried himself off, and put his prison clothes back on, certain he was being watched. He didn't care. He had become used to a lack of privacy. Five minutes later, the door opened, and the two guards came into the room followed by a short, chubby, middle-aged Hispanic woman carrying a black tray on which sat a plastic plate with a clear plastic cover. On top of the tray was something wrapped in plastic and a small plastic bottle of water. She placed the tray of food on the table and immediately left the room followed by the two guards.

Roger walked over to the table and lifted the plastic cover from the plate. Underneath was a large slab of meat loaf, a large scoop of mashed potatoes, and a small mound of green beans. Simple food. He unwrapped the plastic wrap, and a plastic fork was inside. No knife. No spoon. Roger sat down and ate.

The meat loaf wasn't nearly as good as his mother's. The government meat loaf was bland and had little ketchupy adornment or onions bits. But it was passable as food. The mashed potatoes were stiff, tepid, and obviously instant potatoes coming from a box. The green beans almost assuredly came from a can. No matter. It was food, and Roger was hungry. He finished the food within five minutes, downing it with the water. Nothing to do, Roger decided to go to bed and sleep as long as possible.

Looking for light switches to turn off, Roger realized there wasn't any. Of course. He was still a prisoner not entitled to privacy. A small metallic box was affixed high on the wall opposite the bed. Another was attached to a wall to the right of the bed and another to the left of the bed. Certainly security cameras. He would sleep watched by prison personnel.

Roger dropped to his knees beside the bed, crossed himself, and began to say the Rosary. He wasn't sure what day it was, so he decided to say the Sorrowful Mysteries. He spoke in a whisper. Halfway through the Apostle's Creed a voice from the wall commanded sharply, "Silence, Mr. Lee. Prisoners are not permitted to speak unless questioned by a member of the staff. Is that understood?"

Roger looked at the wall, shook his head, and got underneath the covers. He began to think the Rosary, said it silently in his mind, and finished it a short while later. Roger was tired and worn by strain and knew he would be sleeping very soon. Now at ease and comfortable in a warm bed, Roger fell into a deep sleep.

Roger wasn't sure how long he had slept but guessed he had been sleeping about ten hours. It was his first pleasant night of sleep in many days. How many days had it been since his arrest? It had to have been a week, adding whatever time he spent in the hospital having his face stitched. Was it more? Roger couldn't accurately guess. The days had blended one into the other. Roger rose and went into the bathroom, relieved himself, and took a shower. By the time he had dried himself and slipped his clothes back on, two new guards entered the room. They stood near the door, and Roger sat on the bed. Two minutes later a large, very heavy Black woman with short blond-dyed hair entered with a tray. On the tray was a plastic bowl of cereal, a small container of milk, and a plastic spoon. No coffee.

The Black woman left the room. One of the guards, a very tall, powerfully built Black man of about thirty said, "Be ready to go to the interrogation room in one hour." The two guards left the room while Roger sat and ate his spare breakfast.

An hour later, Roger was back down the hall in the same room where he was interrogated the previous day. The three doctors were there as well. Roger was led to a chair facing the three doctors like yesterday, and he sat. Dr. Longchamp sat back in his chair, and his attitude was pensive. Dr. Yezhov stared Roger's way but betrayed little emotion. Dr. Defarge seemed ill at ease and nervous. She brushed her hair back from her forehead three or four times and tapped her thin chin two or three times. She looked away from Roger when he looked at her. Roger looked at Dr. Yezhov a moment and then looked back at Dr. Defarge. She had been looking at him but turned her head as soon as his eyes met her eyes. Not a good sign. Dr. Defarge looked over at Dr. Yezhov, nodded, took a quick look at her laptop, and looked at Roger. She frowned.

"Mr. Lee, yours is a most difficult case. Most people we question in this room try to hide their reactionary and incorrigible views. You have not. And your views are incorrigible in the eyes of the government authorities and to the three of us who were invested with the power to interrogate you and determine what response the government should take in rehabilitating you. Without a doubt, your views are backward and reactionary. Repulsive to the modern mind. Mr. Lee, you were too honest for your own good. You do realize that?"

"Yes. Being honest was a pretty stupid thing to do," Roger replied.

"Are you willing to change your views?" asked Dr. Defarge.

"How can I change my views and be honest with myself? No." Dr. Yezhov's eyes blazed at Roger from across the room.

Dr. Defarge brushed at the hair around her left ear and continued. "The government provides resorts where people with reactionary, antimodern views can be rehabilitated. The government, in its wisdom, realizes that many people, usually those who grew up in backward, rural parts of the country, are prone to have views intolerable to what the state believes desirable. Older people who are distant from the popular culture are most apt to have intolerable views. The state does not fault rural folk who have unacceptable views, but the state wishes to reform these people and assist in making them better, happier citizens. The government authorities wish to be benevolent and don't want to punish people with reactionary views. Do you understand, Mr. Lee?"

"Yes. I understand what you are saying. I don't like it, but I understand what you are saying."

"Your tone is disrespectful to Dr. Defarge," said Dr. Yezhov, anger in his voice. He sat forward in his chair. Roger glanced at Dr. Yezhov.

"I didn't mean to sound disrespectful. If I seemed to be," said Roger, "I am heartily sorry. I wouldn't want to be disrespectful to a lady."

"Quaint," replied Dr. Defarge with a short smile. "But I am a doctor who happens to be a woman and am certainly not what you would call a lady in any way. My personal feelings are not important or relevant to this process in any case. What needs to be determined is whether you are willing to attend one of these government resorts. The rooms are spacious. The food is very good. Top chefs. Each guest is given their own room with their own computer to surf the Internet. The resorts are placed in some of the most scenic areas of the country. The ocean. Northern lakes. Even the mountains. It would be your choice on where to go. The regimen is for three months, and most guests are most pleased with the amenities of the resorts. These resorts usually have two or three presentations each day that require attendance, but most attendees find these presentations to be helpful in accepting a new worldview. Most guests don't even want to go back to the real world after their three months are up. Mr. Lee, would you consent to being a guest at one of these resorts?"

Roger was nervous. A sense of survival entered his mind. Surrender, accept a three-month sentence at some brainwashing resort, and live the remainder of his life in some sort of half freedom. Perhaps he could go back to growing apples on his farm and isolate himself after he went through reeducation. His current nightmare could be brushed under the rug, and he could fish and hunt and have good times with his friends. Certainly going to one of the resorts offered by Dr. Defarge was the wisest thing for him to do. He could fake the brainwashing, just repeat what he was told by the brainwashers, and return to his mountain farm and return to his true beliefs. It wasn't like lying to the authorities was lying at all. The modernist authorities were dishonest, and their world vision was based on lies and dishonorable intentions. Accept the brainwashing and personal safety seemed assured. But a different notion swept Roger's brain. He would be betraying his own freedom of thought if he accepted the brainwashing resort. He would be surrendering his intellectual freedom and what he believed was true or untrue. And Roger was sure that his view of life was true and that the modernist world Dr. Defarge and Dr. Yezhov represented was untrue. If Roger accepted the invitation to go to a government resort, Dr. Defarge and Dr. Yezhov could say that they had won, and Roger had lost.

"These resorts you speak of, Dr. Defarge, seem like reeducation camps. How am I to be reeducated?" said Roger.

"I would rather not think of them as reeducation camps," replied Dr. Defarge. "I would think of these camps as a positive guidance to those who visit them. And you do need a positive guidance in the new world in which you inhabit. Wouldn't you agree, Mr. Lee?"

"I was content with my old beliefs, however much those beliefs are despised by the national authorities."

"Why don't you just give in, Mr. Lee?" asked Dr. Yezhov.

"I don't know why. It would be easier to just give in. But it is against my nature to support beliefs I don't believe in."

"You are very stubborn, Mr. Lee," said Dr. Defarge.

"I suppose so, Doctor," replied Roger.

"Mr. Lee, we have bent over backward so that you can attend a government resort and be restored to the national ethos that we all must follow," said Dr. Yezhov. "We have tried. You have failed to comply. You reject the modern way of living. That is your choice, is it not?"

"I can't live by lies," Roger answered.

"Then you will be punished for being honest," replied Dr. Yezhov.

Dr. Defarge pushed a button to her left and spoke in a hushed voice. She listened intently, shook her head, and spoke again. She glanced over at Dr. Yezhov and smiled shortly. The conversation with the person on the other end of the phone ended.

"That will be all for today," announced Dr. Defarge.

Roger was led away by two guards. But instead of being led to Room 828, Roger was led to an elevator. The elevator headed down, passing the first floor and heading into the lower levels of the building. He was going back to where he had first been confined. The elevator opened, and he was back into the bleak dungeon of the security police. He was led to a cell where a short, swarthy man with a small card waited. He used the card to open the door and pointed in with his finger. Roger was back in the dreary cell that he had been kept when he first came to the security police headquarters.

Roger sat on the same hard bench and stared about the cell, knowing he was being watched. He was hungry but knew that he could not expect food any time soon. Security police did not care that suspects or prisoners went without. And yes, Roger knew that he was most likely not a suspect in the eyes of the security police, but he was now a prisoner. Roger sat silently, knowing that he had earned the wrath of the security apparatus, especially that part that made the decisions.

Hours of fear and boredom went by. Roger damned himself for his honesty. Why was he so stubborn? Why did he not lie and go with the flow and adapt himself to his questioners? Dr. Defarge gave him an opening. Why not take it? Roger couldn't take the offer because the concept of resorts used to reprogram inmates was unacceptable. Being reprogrammed seemed to be a worse sentence than imprisonment. He would lose his dignity if he had given in to the offer of going to a reprogramming resort. He would have lost his brain and soul if he consented to be rehabilitated by the government. He would no longer be the person he was with fifty-seven years of life experiences, the many happy times and even the occasional defeats, losses, and sorrows. No. He was right to be honest. Being reprogrammed would be worse than death.

Roger's mind churned over and over the idea that he was going to be imprisoned for a long time and perhaps for the rest of his life. Perhaps he would be executed. Official executions had ended years before but that would not keep the security state from dispensing undesirable enemies of the security state. And he was sure that he was now considered an enemy of the security state. That was why he was back in his original cell, sitting on a hard bench.

Roger did not know how long he slept. He was shaken awake by a middle-aged, balding, chunky white guard. Two guards, both young, athletic Black men, stood on either side of the bench. Roger slowly raised himself to sit.

"Get up and follow me," ordered the guard who shook him.

Roger stood and walked behind the white guard, the two other guards following behind Roger. The four men stepped out the cell door and out into the hall. The hall was more crowded than Roger had ever seen it, with other security guards going about their jobs. The atmosphere was almost jovial, with some of the men engaging in small talk and short laughs. A tall Black guard with a gold tooth looked Roger's way and grinned. He looked over at a middle-aged white guard in short sleeves. The white guard sported large tattoos on each forearm. He looked at Roger and then at the tall Black guard. Both chuckled, and the white guard said something under his breath to the tall Black guard. Was it "fresh meat?"

Roger and his three guards walked down the hall to an elevator. The lead guard pushed the button on the wall, and the elevator arrived. The four men entered the elevator. Roger saw the white guard push the number seven on the elevator panel. So Roger was not going for further investigation. What was on the seventh floor?

The elevator opened, and the four men walked out in the hall-way filled with medical personnel. It could have been the hallway of a city hospital. Nurses wearing green scrubs predominated. Most were women under the age of forty. Some wore green scrub hats as well. The doctors wore white medical coats. There were about as many women doctors as men. A tall reception desk where an older, very heavy Black woman sat was a short walk to the right of the elevator. The white guard led the men to the desk.

"I have a patient by the name of Roger Lee with me. Which room should we take him to?" asked the white guard.

The receptionist looked at her laptop for a moment, not find-ing Roger's name right away. She tapped away on the screen with her right hand, and Roger noticed very long, purple-painted false fingernails on the receptionist. She became annoyed and said to the guard, "Nobody by the name of Rogers is expected for medical ser-vices today." She glared angrily at the guard.

"No. His last name is Lee. His first name is Roger," replied the guard.

"Why didn't you tell me the first time?" shot back the reception-ist. The guard did not respond. "Room 726," said the receptionist.

"Thank you," replied the guard. He turned to Roger and the other two guards. "Room 726. Follow me."

Room 726 was a small room with three chairs and what appeared to be a nursing station. One chair faced the other two, and the guards led Roger to that chair. At the opposite end of the room was a door. After a ten-minute wait, three women walked into the room from the back door. The first was a nurse of about thirty wearing green scrubs. She was of medium build, a little overweight, and wearing a scrub hat. Next out the back door was a severe woman who looked in her midforties. She had close-cropped auburn hair and wore a white doctor's coat with black slacks underneath. Last through the door was Dr. Defarge. The two doctors sat on the two chairs facing Roger while the nurse walked over to the nurses' station at one side of the room.

"Mr. Lee, let me introduce you to Dr. Pankhurst. She is going to be your surgeon," said Dr. Defarge. Dr. Pankhurst nodded, showing no emotion.

"I didn't know I was going to have any surgery. I feel quite well," said Roger testily.

"You may feel well, but you are not," answered Dr. Defarge. "Mr. Lee, with your indefensible and contemptible beliefs, you are outside the bounds of modern civilization. As a wise woman said many years ago, you and your ilk are deplorables. People like you are a cancer to the new society that has been built over the last few decades."

"So I have no physical ailment?" Roger asked.

"No. For your age, you are in physically fine shape," said Dr. Pankhurst curtly.

"So what kind of surgery is being proposed?" asked Roger, fidgeting in his chair.

Dr. Defarge paused a second, inhaled and said, "It is important to the security of the state that you do not reproduce. So you are going to have a surgery performed on you that makes it so you are incapable of reproducing."

A wave of shock flowed through Roger's mind. His mind seared red a moment, and he took a deep breath. The he replied, "My wife died only a few months ago. At age fifty-seven, I doubt if I will ever remarry or father any more children."

"That is probably true," Dr. Defarge answered. "But there is a chance you might have sex with a woman who is fertile. The state wouldn't want that if it could prevent that. But there is another reason for the operation."

"Are you going to perform a vasectomy on me?" asked Roger.

"No," replied Dr. Defarge. She brushed her hair back from her left ear with her right hand.

"Am I to be chemically castrated?" Roger asked.

"No."

"Physically castrated?"

"No."

A short smile formed on Dr. Defarge's lips and she shook her head like a first-grade teacher telling a child that his answer to a spelling problem was wrong. Her demeanor was one of restrained delight.

"Mr. Lee, you are to be completely emasculated. You are to have your testicles and your penis removed. You are going to be given an artificial plastic tube as a urethra. The security state believes it is vital that you be emasculated and your manhood taken away from you. White men with independent thoughts that are beyond the bounds of our society are a threat to the progress of modern civilization."

"That is barbarous," replied Roger. He was shaking uncontrollably. Dr. Defarge had the look of suppressed amusement on her face. She seemed happy at the fear that welled up in Roger.

"No, Mr. Lee, you are the barbarian," answered Dr. Defarge. "As another very wise woman said a long time ago way back in the sixties, white men are the cancer of the human race."

Roger paused a moment, took a breath, and replied, "But white men have invented over the last five hundred years almost everything worth inventing."

"So they have," admitted Dr. Defarge, and she smirked. "But their inventions are just truisms today. Edison. Bell. Ford. Gates. They are of little consequence today. What they invented is taken for granted, and the average person wouldn't know them from the latest rapper or actress. Better said, white men invented all these machines, but now the white man isn't really needed. They are an anachronism. The new world will only need the inventions of women and people of color. The inventions of the future will not be of the sort that Edison came up with. The inventions of the future will be largely social inventions. Feminism. The social dominance of women and people of color. The white male will recede in importance." Dr. Defarge smiled broadly and shrugged. "The white male will go to the back of the bus, in that phrase of old."

Roger turned from his chair and pointed at the two black guards at the door behind him. "So they will retain their masculinity? Or will they be emasculated like me?"

"No. They will be encouraged to retain their masculinity. Men like those two guards will be encouraged to have as many children as possible with as many women as possible as long as the women wish their company. The Black man has been abused for centuries. In the future, the Black man will enjoy the boundless joys that were denied them for so long." Dr. Defarge smiled again and continued. "They will enjoy the pleasures of women of all races, and they will enjoy the forbidden fruit denied them for centuries. Children will be born and we will have the rise of the biracial child at first, and then in a century or so, most of the children will be of many races. Black. Brown. Yellow. Red. And the white man will be at the bottom of that future."

"What makes you think that you and the state can micromanage human relations to the degree you wish to do so?" asked Roger.

"Because we have the power," replied Dr. Defarge. "It's a simple as that." Dr. Defarge looked to her left at the nurse at the nursing station and nodded. The nurse began to walk toward Roger with a syringe in her right hand. The older white guard and the two Black guards restrained Roger in his chair. The uniform of his right arm was rolled up forcibly by the white guard and exposed. The nurse disinfected a spot on Roger's right arm and applied the shot. Roger shook for a second and then dropped his head forward and lost consciousness.

Roger woke up in pain many hours later. He was flat in his hospital gurney, and various tubes were all about. A monitor to his right provided many numbers, none of which Roger understood. An IV was stuck in his right arm. Roger fought nausea, and he guessed he didn't vomit because he had no food or drink for so long that he had nothing to vomit. He felt sharp pain at the center of his body. He considered his circumstances. How did it come to this? Why? Days ago—was it weeks ago? (time meant nothing when you were in prison)—he was a free man minding his business and enjoying life. Now he was in pain. His mind was fogged. He looked ahead and saw women in green scrubs walking about. He could hear voices but couldn't hear well enough to know what was being said. It took several minutes, but the fog gradually began to lift like the morning fog on the river in the summer. Roger became more aware of his situation. He had been operated on. His pain centered on his manhood. He slowly moved his left hand down his body toward his middle. He crossed his upper stomach and his belly button. He continued. There was not the usual hair below his stomach. But the nurse had assuredly shaved him for the operation. Roger stopped exploring for a moment, and fear shot through his mind. Was he ready for the truth? The answer was no for at least a minute. He dreaded the truth. For a moment he was a coward, afraid of what might come next. A minute became two minutes and then became three minutes. And then courage seeped back into his mind. Dr. Defarge had told him of what type of operation the government had in store for him. Evil Dr. Defarge. She was happy in telling him of the operation that would end in his emasculation. He moved his left hand a little more, an inch or so. And then another inch. And another. What he should have been able to touch wasn't there. Nothing that was of his body. Just sutures and some sort of plastic tube in his groin that was attached to a large tube that extended from his body and into a plastic container hanging above his right knee. So this was it? Tears ran down his face as he contemplated his mutilation. He suppressed crying, and he almost succeeded. But not totally. He cried and he felt ashamed. He tried to stop crying, but he couldn't stop for what seemed to be a full minute. His gut hurt, not because he was nauseous, but because he had lost self-control. And then he stopped crying and regained control of his emotions. He had lost much of his manhood, but he was still alive.

The medication the nurses pumped through him kept Roger in a daze for several more hours. He would sleep a while, wake for a while in throbbing pain, and then he would fall asleep again. It was often a half sleep, and he would hear muffled, feminine voices and the sound of soft shoes walking about and an occasional beeping sound from the monitor overhead. A bedpan was changed once, but the nurse made the change quickly and effortlessly. Occasionally a guard would mill about outside his room to check up on him. Roger thought that Dr. Pankhurst had come by his room three or four times to check on his condition. Once he saw Dr. Defarge talking with Dr. Pankhurst outside the door to his room.

As best Roger could determine, he spent about three days in recovery. He began to eat light food toward the end of his recovery, Jell-O and pudding, but he really wasn't much interested in eating even though he was physically hungry. He pondered how long he would be kept in recovery. Would he be imprisoned after his recovery was complete? Or would he be released since he was emasculated? Perhaps he would be detained indefinitely or even executed to prevent him from telling other people back home about his ordeal. Or would the security state even care about Roger telling others of his ordeal? Rural people in the mountains meant nothing to the security state. Mountain people were not a threat. They were born, they loved and hated, they worked, they went to church, they had children, they drank and ate and smoked, they hunted and fished, they lived obscure lives far from political power, and they died. Nobody back home would believe him anyway, and he certainly didn't want his neighbors to know that he was no longer fully a man.

One morning—at least it seemed like morning because Roger was fed an English muffin with a small package of industrialized grape jelly—Roger was visited by Dr. Defarge and Dr. Pankhurst. Dr. Pankhurst was dressed in a white lab coat while Dr. Defarge wore a mauve blouse and black dress slacks that revealed a nearly formless stick figure. He was seated upright in his gurney. Outside the door was a guard, a short, skinny man who appeared to Roger to be Filipino.

"Your operation appears to be a success," said Dr. Pankhurst. "Your wounds are healing very nicely. No infection that I can see. I have conferred with the other pertinent doctors on the staff, and they concur that you are on the way to a rapid recovery. You will be able to urinate on your own, and you will probably find that your urination to be more regular and consistent than you had before the operation. So the staff is very pleased with the outcome of the operation."

"But I did not want the operation," replied Roger.

"You gave us no alternative," snapped Dr. Defarge. "We proposed reeducation and rehabilitation, and you refused. We bent over backward to save you from an operation, but you refused to meet us halfway."

"It shouldn't be in your power to force emasculation on a man," Roger replied. Dr. Pankhurst looked at Dr. Defarge nervously.

"But the powers that be granted it to us in the defense and security of our modern state. And the point is moot anyway. You have no testicles. You have no penis. Whatever sexual pleasure you once had is now over. Over because the government wanted it to be over. Your masculinity was considered a threat to the state, so your masculinity was eliminated. How do you like it? You will have to adapt," Dr. Defarge replied, and she smiled.

"I despise my mutilation. I despise the government that ordered it. And I despise you."

"Then we did the right thing in emasculating you." Dr. Defarge gave a short laugh that ended in a giggle. "The world dominated by the white man is over. The white man has ruled for centuries. And now that rule is over. Get used to it, Mr. Lee. It is going to be a woman's world in the future run by women for the benefit of all. It is going to be a more collectivized world. A feminine socialism will be the prevailing focus of the government. Fierce competition is out. Feminine cooperation is in. It will be a softer, nurturing world where the feminine mindset is dominant. A therapeutic governance will be the norm."

"Who will do the muscular work that women are unable to perform?" asked Roger.

"Like plumbing and lumberjacking and construction work and trash collecting?" asked Dr. Defarge with a short chuckle. "Men will retain those sorts of jobs. But at the direction of feminine authority. You can be assured of that."

"What you want is not only insane, it is undesirable."

"From your point of view, perhaps. But not from the feminine point of view. And there are more women than men. When you add the power of women to the power of men of color, the LBGQTIP community, and the white men with low testosterone, you have an irresistible power that will crush the white man. You can be assured of that, too."

There was silence in the room for several seconds. Dr. Pankhurst and Dr. Defarge looked at each other a moment, and Roger looked at them. Dr. Pankhurst was the medical doctor, and Dr. Defarge was the doctor with political power. Dr. Defarge ranked above Dr.

Pankhurst, although Dr. Pankhurst cut into people's bodies and had taken years to hone her skills while Dr. Defarge just toyed with people's brains and pursued an ideological agenda. That was the new world advocated by Dr. Defarge, a world in which skill and work deferred to political power.

"Mr. Lee," said Dr. Defarge finally. "You will be released tomorrow. Dr. Pankhurst will examine you one last time tonight. If she declares you healthy, you will be permitted to leave this institution. You can go home."

"How generous," Roger replied with a grunt. "How am I to get home? I last saw my truck on the Eastern Shore of Maryland. Do I get my truck back?"

Dr. Defarge shook her head. "I know of no truck. And I have no information of what happens to the property of detained suspects such as yourself. What happens at the lower level of the security police is none of our affair at the upper levels of the security apparatus. I wouldn't even know where your wallet is or where your driver's license is. Your money was probably taken by the arresting officer or transportation officers or the booking officer. It is kind of a bonus for them when a suspect is arrested. That's what I've been told."

"Am I to believe that I have lost my truck, my wallet, my driver's license, my cash and my clothes?" asked Roger.

"Yes."

"Did I lose all my rights when I got arrested?"

"Need I answer?" replied Dr. Defarge with a chuckle. "Yes, you lost your old rights when you were arrested. Once you were considered a security risk, you lost your rights. The ancient Bill of Rights has been made more flexible with regards to security risks."

"I don't remember the citizens of the country being asked about having a security state that could take away your rights?"

"You remember correctly, Mr. Lee. The people of the country were never consulted on having a security state. The security of the state is too vital to have to ask the people to vote for it. The security state has been implemented from above by officials better able to analyze security than your average citizen."

"Yet we still have elections," Roger noted.

"Yes, we still have elections. It is important for people to feel like they live in a democracy. But elections are like mascara to paint up the reality of the modern system. In reality, our leaders, many of them unelected, make the policies they think most wise without consulting the voters. And the security of the state is the paramount duty of the state."

"And somehow a simple apple grower from the mountains who wanted to buy some crabmeat was a security risk to the state?" asked Roger, his voice sarcastic.

"That's right. The combination of you wanting to buy crabmeat, a delivery only distributed by the state, and your having a bumper sticker that had a Confederate flag on it brought up red flags on the main computers at the security headquarters in Arlington."

"And why was I emasculated?"

"That was my call. Your views were decidedly reactionary and patriarchal. And we can't have that. We had you in our grasp and decided 'Why not?'"

"Why not. You are a terrible woman."

"From where you are sitting." The room was silent. Dr. Defarge took two steps backward. "Mr. Lee, best of luck. Have a good day." Dr. Defarge turned and left the room.

That was the last Roger saw of Dr. Defarge. Dr. Pankhurst visited two hours later and gave him a perfunctory check. And she was gone, never to be seen again.

Later that night, Roger was roused from his hospital bed. A nurse deattached his IV and monitors. Four armed guards watched from the room's entryway. This was it. Somehow, it was bizarre to think of himself as a free man. He had been a prisoner of the state for what seemed to be at least three weeks, but he couldn't be sure because one day had run into another. He was hungry and felt weak. Roger longed for a beer.

"Follow us," said one of the guards. The man was Hispanic and of medium height and somewhat stocky. His manner was that of a bored person doing something he had done hundreds of times before and would do hundreds of times in the future. The other three guards were young Black males, tall and athletic. Roger did as he was ordered, walking behind the lead guard but just ahead of the junior guards.

They took an elevator deep into the bowels of the building and entered a cavernous loading zone. The loading zone was heavily lit. Two heavyset, middle-aged Black men sat inside a glass-enclosed kiosk with monitors and pass cards strewn about a table. A white van was the only vehicle in the loading zone, and its back door was open wide. Roger saw a bench inside the van and noticed the rear of the van was caged. This was going to be Roger's trip out of confinement.

"Put your hands out in front of you, so I can cuff you," ordered the Hispanic guard. He unfastened the cuffs off his belt and cuffed Roger. The guard pointed inside the van. "Step inside the vehicle and take a seat on the bench."

Roger lifted his left leg into the van but tapped his right leg on the bumper and sprawled forward into the van onto his cuffed hands and his face. Roger could feel a trickle of blood from his right nostril. But he uprighted himself and sat on the bench. The guards laughed at Roger's clumsiness.

"Clumsy old man," said the Hispanic guard, chuckling. He slammed the doors shut, and two minutes later the van drove off through a large doorway and out of the building.

The van cell had only a small oval window for Roger to gaze out, and this window was more for the two guards in the rear passenger seat to keep an eye on Roger. Roger could see that the two guards in the back were two of the guards who had walked him to the van from the hospital room. A burly Hispanic man drove while a very large white man with close-cropped blond hair sat beside the driver. It was dark outside, but there was heavy traffic on the road, and scores of headlights and brake lights abounded. The van stopped at red lights, sat motionless for two minutes, and then drove on. This kind of pace went on for about a half hour until Roger could tell that they were on a major highway, perhaps Route 66.

From the small window, Roger saw mostly darkness with a scattering of automobile and truck lights mixed in with the occasionally lit exit sign. The van drove for at least an hour in what Roger guessed was the Virginia Hunt Country with its undulating, but not very tall, hills. After an hour, the hills became closer to what a person would call a mountain. Eighteen-wheelers sometimes blasted by the van. Roger noticed that it had begun to rain.

Roger noticed the van curl sharply to the right and assumed the van was going north. They might be on 81 going north now. Fifteen minutes went by when the van exited the highway. They came to a set of lights and stopped. When the light turned green, the van turned left, passed through another set of lights, and onto another highway. Route 37, maybe. They exited again five minutes later and turned to the left. Perhaps Route 50. They drove through a set of lights, passed a shopping center, drove through another set of lights, and were into a rural land. Two minutes out in the country, the van pulled over to the side of the road. All four men got out of the van, and Roger heard murmuring between the men. Dark thoughts swept through Roger's mind. Was he going to be executed on the side of the road? No. Why go through the trouble of emasculating him just to execute him a few days later? It would have been a waste of an operation and a surgeon's skills. Then again, almost everything Roger experienced these last few weeks reeked of government arrogance and bureaucratic authoritarianism. There was also bureaucratic dysfunction to consider. In a bureaucracy like that that Roger experienced, one department of the security state might not know, or even care to know, what another department had in its plans. People like Dr. Defarge had little dealings with the guards. They had bureaucratic intermediaries to do that. And how many layers of intermediaries did an organization like the security state have? Probably several.

The back door opened. "Step out," ordered the large white man. Roger did so. It was still raining. The large guard turned the key on Roger's cuffs, and Roger's hands were free.

"You're a free man," said the Hispanic driver. "Get going. We're out of here."

"You're just going to leave me here on the side of the road in the rain?" Roger asked.

"Yup. We're not a taxi service," said the large white guard. "Go where you want to go. You're free. A free man, if you can consider yourself a man." All four guards laughed heartily. They knew what had been done to Roger. Of course they knew.

"Let's get out of here out of this rain," said the Hispanic driver. "I'm hungry and it's getting late." The four men stepped back into the van and drove off. The van U-turned back to the east. Roger watched until the taillights were lost a half mile below a hill, and the van was gone from sight.

Roger walked west on the side of the road. The rain was harder now. He passed an occasional house, lights on inside, but Roger didn't stop. He didn't know anyone on the main road and didn't want to bother anyone this late at night. Roger guessed it was late in the evening and close to midnight. But Roger's sense of time was poor. An occasional car passed him as he walked, and the occasional car came from the east from the mountains. But not many.

The rain became stronger as he walked. Roger began to feel cold, and his thin government clothes were saturated. A wind picked up, and Roger felt colder the closer he got to the mountains. The road was slowly rising, its incline very gradual but consistent. Roger's legs were weary, and his groin ached, but he couldn't stop now. The gravel and rocks on the side of the road hurt his feet. The booties did not offer much protection. He knew home was fifteen miles away, up in the mountains. He had to keep going. Getting home was the goal, and his current misery didn't matter.

He was still in Virginia when the mountain road became very steep. An 18-wheeler passed him, slowing down at the rise of the mountain, and struggled at the climb. The driver put his blinkers on as he slowly rose up the mountain. This rise was the first of three before Roger would reach his mountain-valley home.

Roger continued to tire as he rose up the mountains, and his groin continued to hurt. He passed houses, some with lights on and some without. He didn't stop. Not that most of the people wouldn't give help. Most would. But he didn't want to wake them up. He wanted to get back to his home on his own without the help of others. He was stubborn and foolish. But he was thinking that his nightmare was ending, and he would return to a gentler, more civilized world. It would be all right soon.

He went down the first slope and began to cramp in his left leg. Sometimes going down a mountain was harder on the legs than going up. Roger stopped for thirty seconds and lifted his left leg for five seconds and placed it back on the ground. He did it two more times, and the cramp eased. He continued to walk. Roger reached the bottom of the mountain, and then he was walking up the next slope.

The road snaked all the way up the mountain. Left. Right. Left. Right. Left and then up. A truck came from the west up the crest, and he could see the driver's face in the window outlined by the truck's headlights. The truck passed, and Roger could hear the truck hit gravel on the side of the road at the turn going the other way.

Down the second slope went Roger. The rain continued to pour hard, but it didn't matter because Roger was already at maximum absorption. Rain in his hair slid off his head and into his eyes and mouth. His ears were cold. Every step he took, Roger could feel cold water rise from the bottom of his bootie, up into his saturated socks, and out the bootie. Holes had developed in both booties. His feet were cold but warmer than the rest of his body. They were doing work. His feet were active.

A car passed Roger from behind, the driver slamming down on his horn as he passed. Roger had surprised the driver. Normally, nobody would be walking on this road in the rain at night. The driver screamed something out his window, but Roger couldn't comprehend what the driver said. The driver never slowed down, and Roger kept walking and soon was down the second slope.

The road curved back and forth for a mile, but the elevation varied little now. Roger was entering a familiar section of the county. On the right was Miller's ice cream parlor, a popular place in the summer. It was never open after the middle of October and wouldn't open again until April. Soon he could see the old Henry farmhouse. Bill and Doris still lived in the old house, but they were in their eighties and didn't keep animals any longer. Roger didn't see lights on in the house. Three hundred yards further along was the Bright farm, and he could hear the bleating of sheep in the far distance. The

Brights kept their sheep outdoors whenever the weather was mild. The Brights had small shelters for the sheep to get out of the rain.

Roger reached the foot of Bear Claw Mountain, and he was feeling satisfied. His feet hurt and his groin hurt and he was soaked to the bone, but he was close to home. The bad dream was ending. And a thought came into his head. Would his neighbors believe his story? Should he even tell them? They would certainly puzzle at why he was gone from home for so long. Were his five dozen chickens still alive? They would have long been out of water or feed. And his sheep? Would his friends and neighbors understand how the government elites and its security state considered all the people of the mountains as potential enemies and whose views were despicable? Most knew it, but the government was distant, so this dislike for them did not permeate the society of the mountains. Roger's experience with the government was something new.

The mountain road wound sharply left, and the rise was sharp. The left curved lasted two hundred yards. There were no houses on the road now, only a forest of trees, scrub pine, pitch pine, red oak, maple, and hickory. The rain was coming down even harder, but that mattered very little to Roger. He was close to home. Then the curve wound hard right, and the gradient was even steeper. Roger struggled but went on. He had made it this far. He had only a little farther to go. Just tell your brain to step and then step again and then step again. Keep stepping and don't stop.

Roger noticed that the complete darkness of his walk was losing out to the early light of day as he reached the summit of Bear Claw Mountain. He came up to an abandoned house that had been falling apart for as long as Roger could remember. Roger didn't even know who had owned it in the past. The house had no window glass, and most of the shutters were gone but one that sat on an angle from a top floor window. The front door had lost its paint but still barred entry to the house. Even when Roger was a boy, the children considered the house haunted.

Roger was now walking sharply down Bear Claw Mountain. There was little shoulder here on the road, and he was worried about traffic behind his back. He thought about crossing the road to face traffic, but that would be foolish. There was no shoulder on the other side, only the sheer cliff of Bear Claw. He would keep as he was.

A truck began climbing the mountains toward Roger. It had its headlights on, and it made a loud, grinding noise as it accelerated up the mountain. The truck passed before Roger as it continued up the mountain. A silver tool chest sat in the back of the truck against the cab. The truck was just one of many that went east from the mountains six days a week to do work where the money was.

Roger kept walking down the mountain. It wasn't far to Stonewall now. The light was stronger now, and the rain began to slacken. And then a last curve and he was on level ground and entering the town. He passed the old familiar places of the town. The Stonewall convenience store. The firehouse. Johnson's Hardware. Jalisco's Mexican restaurant. The Dollar Store. Dr. Osbourne's office. The two banks.

Beth Grayson looked outside the front window of Mike's Diner. They would be opening up for service in a few minutes. Beth saw a man walking in the rain in the direction of the diner. The man was dressed stupidly for being in the rain, and he walked unsteadily. He looked pathetic like a homeless person from the cities to the east. The man approached slowly.

"Will you look at that?" Beth said to Carlyn Davis, who was at the back counter near the cash register, wiping off the plastic covers of the menus. "Ain't it odd that a man is walking in the rain on a morning like today?"

"Could it be a homeless man? Not many come through here, that's for sure. But I've seen some homeless on occasion," answered Carlyn with no concern in her voice. She looked back to the galley where the cook was cutting up potatoes with a paring knife.

"He looks really beat. And he's wearing some sort of orange uniform. Like he's just broke out of jail," said Beth. "He looks pretty old from what little I can see from here."

Beth continued watching the man as he walked up the road toward the diner. He didn't walk fast, but his pace was steady. More light filtered through from the sky, although there was no sun yet and not likely to be any sun that day. And then recognition crossed Beth's consciousness. The man walking in the rain in the orange jump-suit was someone familiar. But it couldn't be. But yes, it was. That bedraggled man was a neighbor and friend. It was Roger Lee.

"My god, it's Roger. Roger Lee. Oh my god," cried Beth Grayson. She bolted out the nearest door and ran toward Roger as he kept walking up the street.

"Roger! Roger! Roger! Stop!" called out Beth as she ran up to Roger, splashing through the wet asphalt. Roger turned to his left and saw a middle-aged, heavyset woman running toward him from across the street. He stopped. He recognized the woman.

"What are you doing? Where have you been? Nobody knew where you went. Where have you been all this time?" said Beth, and she hugged the soaked man. She held his left shoulder and led him across the street and toward Mike's. She led him toward one of the doors of the diner, still holding him by the shoulder where Carlyn and Matt the cook stood. Carlyn was weeping.

Beth and Roger came to the door. "I ain't workin today, Carlyn. Just tell Mike. You gotta handle things today and stop that cryin', Carlyn. I gotta help Roger today. He's badly off, and I gotta help him. I'm takin' him to his house and get him out of these wet clothes."

"Yes, Beth. Of course," answered Carlyn, still crying. "What happened?"

"Don't know. I got to get Roger home. I'll talk to y'all later," said Beth as she led Roger to her car. She opened the passenger door and pushed Roger inside. Beth ran around to the other side, slipped to one knee, rose, got in the car, and drove off. Beth didn't pause for traffic on the main road and sped off to the Lee farm.

"Where ya been, Roger? People knew you went to Maryland for a day or two, but it's been three weeks. We were beside ourselves," said Beth as she barreled down the road. She turned right.

"That was the plan. Just wanted to buy some crabmeat," answered Roger. He was shivering now in the cold car, and Beth noticed.

"Sorry, hun, the car doesn't heat very fast. I'll get ya home," said Beth.

"I'm all right."

"It's like you vanished, Roger," said Beth, and she pulled onto the dirt road to Roger's farm.

"I felt like I vanished, Beth. Nobody would believe where I've been for the last few weeks. Nobody."

The road was the old familiar dirt road with potholes and small tree limbs and sticks and brush. Trees were heavy on the river side, and most of the leaves were down and cluttered about. Roger had left Stonewall when the leaves were at peak color. A fog was forming because of all the rain, the rain returning back to the sky from where it had come and would come again.

They came across the Bradshaw farm on the left. The Bradshaw cattle were off in a field to the left of the house and barn and up a gentle hill. They were eating tall grass that Lou Bradshaw had not hayed. A doe jumped out of a small clump of trees to the right of the Bradshaw house and was followed by an eight-point buck. Roger realized it was rutting season now for the deer. He had missed much while he was away.

Beth drove up the small driveway to the Lee house. She parked and ran around the car to the passenger's side. Roger was part way out, and Beth yanked him up by his right shoulder and to her sturdy, fat body.

"Lean on me, Roger. I'll get ya in the house. Come on, sugar. Lean on me."

Roger obeyed the woman and walked with her to the front door. His knees were weak. The physical stress he had been under was catching up with him now that he had come to a refuge. His fight was over, and his body was shutting down. He was glad to have Beth and her block of a body to help him. The front door was not locked and never was. Beth opened the door and led Roger to a sofa, and Roger collapsed into it and fell asleep.

Beth had been in Roger and Connie's house only a few times, but she quickly figured out which bedroom he slept. It was upstairs. Women figure out a house faster than any man. She found Roger's dresser and pulled out a white thermal shirt and a red-and-green checkered flannel shirt. In a closet, she found a pair of blue jeans. Beth brought the clothes to where Roger slept on the sofa.

Beth unfastened all the snaps of Roger's orange jumpsuit and began to pull his arms out of the sleeves. It was difficult to pull Roger's arms out because the fabric was so wet and stuck to Roger's skin. She pushed the fabric back, yanked his right arm an inch out of the sleeve, pushed again, yanked another inch, pushed again, and then Roger's arm came out easy. Beth pulled the right side of the jumpsuit behind Roger, got a good hold of it, and pulled it toward her. She then pulled the left sleeve, got Roger's arm out to the elbow, and the rest of his arm came out easy.

Beth stood above Roger and looked at him. The skin of his torso was ghost white and scattered with red and purple blotches. It was wet and cold. She went off to the bathroom and returned with a towel to dry Roger off. She dried his chest and arms and face, pulled Roger toward her, and dried his back. She then let Roger fall back onto the sofa, and he grunted softly. She teared for a moment as she looked at him. What had happened to this gentle man? What evil had he gone through?

It was time to pull off the rest of Roger's jumpsuit. It had to be done. Modesty had to be put aside. Beth pulled the back of the suit down past Roger's backside and to his calves. Then she pulled down the front. She did not see what she expected to see. Beth had expected to see what a normal man would have at his middle. But Roger did not have what Beth expected to see. Beth was shocked at what she saw and looked away. She looked again at Roger and looked away again. She turned her head back. A short, stubby tube extended from Roger where his maleness had been. She stood and began to sob. She began to shake uncontrollably and turned her back to Roger and walked to the other side of the room. Unsteady, Beth sat in an easy chair and began to cry.

Tears flowed for several minutes as Beth sat in the chair. What sort of people would do that to a man? And why? Was it the government that had done this to Roger? Or was it some sort of crime organization? How could such a kind, decent man like Roger be so horribly mutilated?

Five minutes of tears went by before Beth gathered herself together. A cold, naked, hurt man lay on the sofa who needed her.

She rose from the chair and began to dress Roger. Beth had difficulty putting clothes on the sleeping body but finally got Roger dressed. Then she searched for a blanket to put over Roger. She found a blanket in Roger's closet and brought it back down the stairs and draped it over Roger. That done, Beth went into the kitchen to brew some coffee. It would be a long time before Roger would wake up and Beth needed coffee to pass the time.

Roger was still sleeping at three o'clock when Carlyn entered the house. "How is Mr. Lee?" she asked as she came upon Beth drinking coffee as she sat in the easy chair.

Beth pointed down the room at Roger sleeping on the sofa. "Roger's sleeping. Be quiet. Let him sleep as long as he wants. He's been through hell. Ah think he was tortured."

"Tortured?" replied Carlyn, and her face was full of shock. She raised her right hand to her forehead.

"Yeah, tortured. He's hurt real bad. Something deliberate was done to him. Something bad was done to him. Real mean. Vicious mean."

"Why?"

"Don't know. He didn't say. Just said that nobody would believe his story. Got him inside the house, plopped him down on the sofa, and he fell asleep. Got him out of his wet clothes and got him into some warm ones. Found a blanket."

"Wonder what he means by nobody would believe his story," said Carlyn and as she glanced down the room at the sleeping man.

"I have an idea why he said that," replied Beth and she became quiet. She began to tear up again, dropped her head into her hands, and began to sob. Carlyn walked over to Beth and placed her right hand on Beth's shoulder. Beth continued to sob. Carlyn leaned down, and the younger woman hugged the older. Carlyn began to tear as she hugged Beth in reaction to Beth's sobbing. She had never seen Beth cry or sob before.

The two women held each other for several moments until Beth's emotional storm subsided, and she quieted. Beth raised her head and looked into Carlyn's eyes.

"You know, ah had to strip Roger out of that wet outfit he had on so he wouldn't freeze to death."

"Of course. You did the right thing. I don't think Mr. Lee would mind you seeing him with his clothes off. There was nothing else for you to do."

"So I saw Roger naked." Beth sobbed a moment, and Carlyn watched. Beth went on. "Something bad was done to Roger. Something really bad. A horrible thing."

"What?"

"Something was done to his man parts. Something evil. Something terribly evil."

"What do you mean?"

Emotion overwhelmed Beth again, and she began sobbing again. Then she abruptly stopped. "Roger's man parts aren't there anymore. Just a tube." Carlyn fell into Beth's lap and began to cry. The two women held each other and cried into each other's arms for several minutes. Beth patted Carlyn about the young woman's back.

Roger moaned from across the room, and he turned on the sofa. He moaned again but went back to sleep. The women stopped crying and watched Roger. When Roger was again silent, the two women looked into each other's eyes, still tearing.

"Did you let anyone know about what happened to Roger?" asked Carlyn.

"The man thing. No. I haven't called no one yet. But I got to get in touch with the Wessingers. They're Roger's best friends. But Matt saw Roger this morning. You know how fast news travels in a town like Stonewall. Probably half the town knows Roger's back. So I need to bring the Wessingers here and talk with Roger. I think I'll drive over to the Wessingers after I give Roger a check now that you're here."

Beth walked over to where Roger slept, went to her knees, and uncovered the blanket from Roger's body. The blue jeans Roger was wearing were wet at the crotch. Beth knew what it was but went through the motions. She touched the wet with her right hand, smelled her fingers, and shook her head at Carlyn standing next to them.

147

"Roger pissed himself, poor man," said Beth. She stood. "Ah'm going upstairs to get Roger some new pants. Carlyn, pull off his pants for me while ah get him some new pants."

"You sure?"

"Yeah," Beth replied and she smiled. "He ain't gonna mind." Beth walked up the stairs to find new pants for Roger.

Carlyn pulled off Roger's blue jeans, saw that he had been mutilated, and began to cry again. She stood, looking away to her left. She could not bear to look at Roger and the tube that came out from where Roger's manhood should have been. She walked away toward the kitchen but did not go in. She just stood there weeping.

Beth returned with another pair of blue jeans. "Come help me, Carlyn. Help me get these blue jeans on Roger. It's not easy lifting a man's body about. Four hands are better than two."

"Okay," replied Carlyn, and she walked back over to where Roger slept on the sofa. The two women pulled Roger's sleeping body into the blue jeans one leg at a time and yanked the blue jeans over the tube. Beth put the blanket back over Roger. Two minutes later, Beth drove off to the Wessingers.

Roger began to wake fifteen minutes after Beth drove off. His dream began to drift from his tired mind. He wanted his dream to remain, fought consciousness, but the dream was gone. But it felt good that he was warm. Something in his mind told him that he was safe now. But where was he? He opened his eyes, saw the familiar room, and realized he was home. He sat up and looked about. Carlyn sat in a chair across the room.

"Hi. Carlyn Baker. Is that you? Glad to see you and surprised to see you. Hi, Carlyn. I'm home, right?"

Carlyn stood and ran to where Roger sat on the sofa. She fell to her knees before Roger and put her arms around the man and collapsed into Roger's body. She hugged Roger and began to cry. Roger allowed Carlyn to hug him and just sat. Carlyn cried a while, and Roger freed his arms to hug Carlyn back.

"Why are you crying?" Roger asked, and he wiped the tears from the young woman's eyes.

"Just happy you're safe," replied Carlyn.

"I am safe. And I am home."

"You are home."

"How did I get here?"

"You forgot?"

"Yes. I forgot."

"Beth saw you walking through town in the rain this morning. She saw you. She drove you home. Don't you remember?"

"No. I don't remember. Maybe I'll remember later. But I can't remember now."

"That's not important. It's important that you are home. You're home with people who care for you. Love you."

"Yes."

"Why were you walking in the rain, Mr. Lee? Do you know why?"

"I don't know right now. I'll try to remember later," Roger replied, and he smiled.

"You were soaking wet. And you were cold and shivering."

"Yes. I must have been soaked. I'm warm now."

"Beth put you in dry clothes. She found some upstairs in your bedroom."

"Oh."

Carlyn fell forward into Roger and began to cry again. Roger held her gently and patted her back lightly. "Easy, Carlyn. Easy, girl. Everything's going to be okay," said Roger, and he continued to pat the young woman on the back.

"Why did," said Carlyn as she pushed herself away from Roger's body, "why did, why did they hurt you?" Tears ran down Carlyn's face in two rivulets. "Why?"

"Because they can," said Roger and Carlyn fell forward again into Roger's body and cried some more, but the crying was quieter as the young woman began to regain her composure.

"Are you in pain, Mr. Lee?"

"Yes. Just a little. But I'll be okay. I can deal with it."

"Why did the people who hurt you do what they did?"

"Because they thought I was some kind of threat."

"So they, so they," said Carlyn, and she couldn't complete her thought. She began to sob quietly.

"So they what?"

"So they did what they did to you."

"Oh. Beth told you. When she put me in warm clothes."

Carlyn fell forward again into Roger's body, and he held her. "I saw too, Mr. Lee. I saw too."

"Oh. I see."

Carlyn was still crying softly against Roger's body when Beth came in the house with Sam and Becca Wessinger. They walked through the open door. The rain had stopped, and the sun was peeking through the clouds and filtering into the room. Carlyn turned to the three at the doorway. Becca placed her right hand across her mouth, said nothing, and ran to Roger. Carlyn stood and allowed Becca by.

"My dear Roger. Oh my. Oh my heaven. You are home, my sweet Roger," said Becca, and she leaned down and kissed Roger on the top of his forehead and then his left cheek. Beth and Sam stood behind Becca. Becca hugged Roger and began to sob lightly for a moment, kissed Roger on his left cheek again, and stood. Sam nodded at Roger and held out his hand and Roger shook it.

"What happened?" Sam asked.

"I don't know. No. I'm just having a hard time remembering. It was like a bad dream," said Roger and Becca placed her right palm on her right cheek. "I think I'll remember soon. But I'm having a hard time thinking right now. A lot of bad things happened to me. A lot of bad things."

The four stood a moment in silence, not knowing how to proceed. How do you talk to a friend who has been brutalized? Should you bring up unhappy subjects? Should you ask questions that reveal a terrible truth? Or do you dummy up and act like the last three weeks never happened?

Roger preferred truth. He looked up at Beth. "Does Becca and Sam know?" Beth shook her head, and her eyes became glassy.

"We know, Roger. We know," said Sam and Becca shook her head. She began to tear and wiped at her eyes. Everyone was silent for a minute.

"Well, how are my chickens?" asked Roger. He smiled.

"Griff took care of them. Collected the eggs. Boxed them and refrigerated them. They're up in one of your barn refrigerators," replied Sam.

"And the sheep?"

"Griff took care of them too," said Sam and he sniffed his nose.

"Fine. I'll have to thank Griff when I see him next," said Roger. "When did you realize I was gone missing?"

"The town realized it when you didn't show up for breakfast the first Saturday you were gone. You're at breakfast nearly every Saturday. It was the buzz around Mike's the whole morning. People were askin' where you were and when they'd seen you last. People called your phone, but there wasn't an answer," said Beth.

"Bobby Strong gave us a call that first Saturday," said Becca. "And we told Bobby we had canned green beans with you the previous Saturday but hadn't seen you since."

"So Becca, Griff, and I drove over to your house," said Sam. "Your best truck was gone. Checked the hens, and they were out of water. We knew something was wrong then and there. Roger Lee wouldn't let his hens go thirsty."

"We knew you have gone to Maryland to buy some crabmeat," said Becca. "We were worried."

Sam said, "So we got in touch with Mac. We asked him to check to see whether you might have gotten in an accident." Sam shook his head. "Mac checked his computer and said there was no accidents involving you in Maryland, Virginia or West Virginia."

"It is like you vanished," said Carlyn.

Becca asked, "Are you hungry, Roger?"

"Sure am. What happened to me is still coming back to me. But I do remember not eating much. I'm very hungry."

"You look hungry," said Becca. "Like you lost a lot of weight. We've got a pot of stew out in the truck." She looked at her husband

and shook her head. "Could you bring it in, Sam? I'll warm it up in the kitchen."

Sam brought in a large blue Dutch oven and followed Becca into the kitchen. There was no door to the kitchen, just a clear walkway. Sam placed the Dutch oven down on the stove, and Becca slid it over to one of the burners and turned the burner on.

"Let's go off to the kitchen," said Roger, and he and the two other women followed.

While the stew cooked, the five of them sat down at the long wooden kitchen table.

Roger looked at Carlyn. "You gave birth. Was it a boy or a girl?"

"A boy. I named him Tanner. Eight pounds, nine ounces."

"Congratulations. That's great news."

"Thanks, Mr. Lee."

"He's a beautiful boy," said Beth. "He's got pretty blue eyes."

"Yes, he does," said Becca.

"Where is he?" asked Roger.

"At my mom's."

"Right," said Roger. "Any news since I was gone?"

"Yancey Richardson died. Drug overdose," said Sam.

"He was never the same after the government closed him down," said Roger.

"No he wasn't. But he had a drug problem before. Not a real bad one," said Sam. "But he did do drugs. Pills. But losing his business brought Yancy down so far. So he did more and more drugs."

Becca walked to a row of cabinets along the wall opposite the stove. The first cabinet did not have what she was looking for, but the second one did. She pulled out ceramic bowls for the five of them and placed the stack of bowls on the counter next to the stove. The stew was beginning to bubble.

"Poor Yancey," said Becca. She found a wooden spoon in a drawer below the counter, stirred the stew, ripped a paper towel from a spool, placed the paper towel on the counter, and took the wooden spoon from the stew and placed it on the paper towel. "I often saw Yancey just sitting in a chair outside his house smoking a cigarette and drinking cans of beer when I drove by his house. Guns were a big part of his life and kept him busy. When the government destroyed his business, he just died inside."

"Ain't that the truth," said Sam.

Becca brought out spoons and placed them in front of the four people sitting and at the place next to Sam. She then grabbed white napkins from a small stack on a counter nearest the refrigerator and put one at the proper place on the table. She found a ladle in a drawer and ladled out stew in a bowl and brought it to Roger. The stew steamed.

"Looks mighty fine, Becca," said Roger.

"Cooked it up yesterday," said Becca, and she filled another bowl and brought it to Carlyn.

"Stew's best the day after it's been made," said Sam.

"That's for sure," said Roger.

"Even the second day after," said Beth.

"Yeah, it thickens as it gets older," said Becca. "Made it with beef. Not deer."

"I like it with both," said Roger. He waited for the rest to get their bowls of stew. Roger made the sign of the cross and said a short prayer.

"Same here," said Sam.

"Never had it with deer meat," said Carlyn.

"Never had deer stew, Carlyn," said Becca. "You'd really like it with deer."

"Yes, you would," said Beth. "My ex-husband liked me to cube the backstrap and make deer stew for him. But that's long ago. I haven't cooked deer stew since Dave left. That's almost ten years ago. He liked deer chili too. I haven't made that in about ten years."

Becca had finished dishing out the bowls of stew and was about to sit down but then remembered that no one had anything to drink.

"Anything in the refrigerator?" she asked Roger.

"Beer and orange juice is about it," Roger answered. "And the orange juice must be rancid by now. I don't usually keep much of any drinks but beer and a container of orange juice. Sometimes a bottle of red wine."

Becca and Sam walked over to the refrigerator. Sam opened the door and Becca gazed inside and saw the bottles of beer to the left and a bottle of red wine on the shelf to the right. The red wine was half full.

"Beer or red wine is your choice," Becca announced.

"I know you want a beer," said Sam, looking over at Roger, as he grabbed two beer bottles from the refrigerator.

"The bottle opener is in the drawer close by the table," said Roger, and he pointed. Sam opened the drawer, found the opener, and snapped off the bottle tops. He came back to the table with two beers.

"I'll take a beer too," said Beth. "Please."

"Fine," said Sam, and he gave Beth a beer and Roger a beer. Becca walked to the table with the bottle of red wine.

Roger pointed at a cupboard to the rear of the kitchen. "The wine glasses are over there."

"What are you drinking?" Sam asked Carlyn.

"Beer is fine," replied Carlyn.

"You sure you're of age?" asked Sam with a short chuckle.

"I'm twenty-three," Carlyn answered.

"Just checking, young lady," said Sam. He pulled out two more beers, opened them, and brought the bottle of beers to the table. Becca found a wine glass, brought it over to the table, and sat. She poured herself a glass of wine, and the five began to eat.

"Roger, where's your truck?" Sam asked.

"Don't know. I was arrested and never saw the truck again."

"Don't they give you back all the things you had when you were arrested?" asked Becca.

"They didn't with me. No truck. No wallet. No money." Roger ate a spoonful of stew, and it was delicious. The beef was tender and easy to eat. The stew had potatoes, carrots, peas, and onion bits in it. The gravy was dark brown.

"The government just can't take your things, can they?" asked Carlyn.

"Apparently they can," Roger answered.

"Oh my," said Becca. "Are you sure they were from the government?"

"They were government. Kept calling themselves security police," said Roger. "I'm remembering more of what happened to me. The cobwebs are shaking some. Yeah. I was arrested on the Shore in Maryland not long after I tried to buy some crabmeat. I was jailed in the town jail by myself. But men with the security police took me from the town jail and drove me to Arlington, Virginia. I remember seeing the Washington Monument out a window." Roger stopped and smiled. "They still call it the Washington Monument, right?"

"Yeah. For now," said Sam. "Congress is thinking of renaming it after Eleanor Roosevelt. We'll see."

"So you were kept in Arlington, Virginia?" asked Beth.

"Yeah. In a cell in the basement at first. I remember it being cold and the bench I had to sit and sleep on was hard, and the food was sparse and tasted bad."

"No phone call to find a lawyer?" said Sam.

"None of that. I do remember them saying that security risks had no rights. That I remember."

"And I thought this was America," said Becca.

"It isn't the old America with the right of the accused."

"So you were considered a security risk, Mr. Lee?" asked Carlyn. "Why?"

"That's coming back to me as well. I wasn't able to buy any crab. It apparently isn't sold to the public any longer. Crabbers still go out and get crab, but the government gets it all and the important people in the government gets the crab. When I was driving home, I was stopped for having a light out on the truck. A tail light. The local cop must have smelled beer on my breath, so he gave me a sobriety test. I passed that and a breathalyzer test and was ready to go when a security cop came up and noticed that Confederate bumper sticker on my rear bumper with the battle flag on it. And he arrested me, and my troubles began."

"Oh my," said Becca.

"And the security police arrested you for a bumper sticker?" asked Sam.

"That's right."

"I've never heard of security police," said Beth.

"I hadn't either. Until about three weeks ago." Roger stopped, drank a sip of beer, and said, "That beer hits the spot. I haven't had a beer since I was arrested."

"I bet it does taste good," said Sam.

"Yes, it does."

"What kind of place was this security prison? asked Sam.

"It is more than a prison. My time there was as a prisoner in a cell. I'd never been in jail before, so it was odd to be a prisoner. You are monitored all the time. Once I began to pray out loud and was ordered to shut up."

"So they didn't even allow you to pray?" asked Becca.

"No. They wanted total silence. I remember that. No speaking unless you were asked a question."

"You must have been scared," said Carlyn.

"Yes. I was. I was scared. I was bored a lot too. Being in a jail cell with nothing to do can be right dull."

Becca looked at Roger with concern, tried to speak, looked away at the stove for a couple seconds. Becca finally asked, "Roger, how do you feel? Are you in pain?"

"I hurt some. But the sleep I had after I got back home has made me feel stronger. Just getting out of wet clothes and out of the rain made me feel better."

"Why did they hurt you?" asked Beth.

"Because I would not compromise my beliefs."

"They asked about your beliefs. That is peculiar," said Becca.

"We're a free country, aren't we?" asked Beth.

"Maybe in theory like how they used to teach it in the schools. But not practically. I was asked a lot of questions by three government doctors. I gave them answers. They didn't like the answers. They said I was a reactionary. They said I was a deplorable."

"Why didn't you lie, Mr. Lee?" asked Carlyn.

"Carlyn, I asked myself the same question. I could have lied and be reprogrammed into being someone other than myself. But I had to be true to myself and accept the consequences."

"What they did to you is so wrong," said Beth. She began to tear.

"Yes. It was wrong what the government did. That's how much the government hates people like us. Maybe that's why they hurt me."

The five of them ate in silence for a while. Roger had talked about his ordeal about as much as he wanted, and the others were reticent to ask too many questions. Becca poured herself more wine, and the others drank their beer.

Becca finally spoke. "Roger, the four of us are the only people who know about your surgery. Do you want it to stay that way?"

"Yes. I don't want anyone else to know."

"Then that's final," said Sam. "Not a word."

Becca stood and walked over to the stove. "Anyone want more stew?"

"No," answered Carlyn. "I have to pick up Tanner from my mom."

"I'm fine," said Beth.

"I could use another bowl," said Roger.

"Make that two," said Sam.

"Haven't had good old home cooking for a while. You never know how much you miss something until it's taken away for a while," said Roger.

"Bad cooks in the government?" asked Sam.

"Yeah. Bad cooks in the government. Can't even make good meat loaf," said Roger. Becca grabbed Roger's bowl, filled it, and brought it back to him. He began to eat. Becca brought her husband more stew.

Carlyn stood, gave Roger a long hug, said goodbye, and left.

Sam spoke. "In a small town like ours, news about your return will travel fast. Probably half the town knows now, and the other half will know within a day or two." Becca shook her head.

"Yeah. I know it. Nothing against my friends and neighbors, but I wish things could be normal again. Like they were a month ago. But they can't be the same," said Roger, and he finished the beer he was drinking.

Sam noticed and asked, "Do you want another, Roger?"

"Sure."

"Get me one too, please," said Beth.

"Sure," said Sam. He rose, walked over to the refrigerator, brought out three beers, opened them, and brought them to the table.

"Do you think the government put into you one of those implants?" asked Becca.

"I don't know," answered Roger. He ate a spoonful of stew.

"What do they call them things?" asked Beth.

"Microchips," said Sam.

"That's right," said Roger as he finished chewing the food. "I think it was originally implanted into criminals. Of course, I am considered a criminal. Who knows whether one was implanted in me when I was unconscious? I was beaten very thoroughly after I was arrested in Maryland."

"Hell, they probably consider all of us in the mountains to be capable of crime against the government," said Sam.

"Yes, they do," said Roger. He was feeling tired as he ate his second bowl of stew.

"Three so-called doctors questioned me," said Roger.

"What do you mean so-called?" asked Beth.

"They weren't medical doctors. Not the kind that examine patients like a real doctor would. They don't take out tonsils or appendixes or do heart surgery or fix someone's hemorrhoids," said Roger and the four of them chuckled. "These three doctors were solely concerned whether I was politically correct and whether I saw the world the same way they did."

"And you don't," said Sam.

"No, I don't."

"And that's why they hurt you," said Becca in a quiet tone of voice. Beth wiped a tear from her right eye.

"Yes, that's why they hurt me."

"Why didn't you lie to the government people?" asked Beth.

"I should have, I guess. It would have been easier, and I wouldn't have been hurt. Mutilated. But I would have been lying to myself if

I didn't answer their questions truthfully. So I told them my truth," said Roger and he drank a swallow of beer. He went on. "A great man of the past said something to the effect that a man who lies to himself and believes his own lies becomes unable to see the truth. He loses respect for himself and for other people. When he loses respect for himself and other people, he loses his humanity. He indulges himself in any impulse and reduces himself to an animal." Roger ate a last spoonful of stew.

"Who said that, Roger?" asked Becca.

"Dostoyevsky," replied Roger. Sam smiled.

"I've never heard of him," said Beth.

"He was a Russian writer from long ago," said Sam. "He's not taught anymore. Not even in college."

"That he's not taught shows how low our civilization has sunk," said Roger. He yawned. "I am getting tired. Do you mind if I stepped over to the sofa?"

The four got up from the kitchen table and walked into the living room sofa. Roger sat at one corner, Beth in the middle, and Becca at the other corner. Sam sat in the chair.

"Do you think they'll ever come for us?" asked Beth.

"No. They don't have the resources. There's too many of us and too few of them. And from what I experienced at the security prison, most of the workers are there for the job and the paycheck and do as little as possible. The average worker was no fanatic. Only the doctors proved to be fanatics." Roger stopped for a moment and continued. "They emasculated me as an example, I suppose. When my story becomes part of common knowledge up here in the mountains, people are going to wonder if what happened to me might happen to them if they get on the wrong side of the government. So hurting me is setting an example."

"They are diabolical," said Sam.

"Yes, they are. With modern technology, the government can be diabolical whenever it wants to bad enough," said Roger.

"That's not a way to live. How can they stand themselves?" asked Becca.

"The people who run the security for the government are true believers. They believe they are right, they are introducing a bright new future, and we are wrong to believe in the old values."

"So they are anti-Christian?" asked Becca.

"Yes, they are anti-Christian," replied Roger and his head fell to his chest, and he released his bottle of beer. He was asleep, and Beth and Becca laid him out on the sofa.

"Better let him sleep," said Becca. "After all Roger's been through, he needs sleep."

"I'll stay tonight," said Sam.

Beth shook her head. "No. I will. I'll just call Kayla and tell her to spend the night next door with the Maxwells. I'll call LaDonna Maxwell, and she will be glad to have Kayla over. Kayla and her granddaughter are best friends at school."

Becca and Sam left Roger's house shortly after. Beth sat in a chair as Roger slept. An hour went by. Roger became restless and tossed about. Beth went over to Roger and patted his head and face. She kissed Roger's left cheek and said, "Go to sleep, Roger. Just sleep. Everything's all right." And Roger calmed down and fell into a deeper sleep and stopped tossing. Beth went back to her chair and soon was sleeping too.

Roger woke at six the next morning and saw Beth sleeping in the chair. He went to the kitchen, brewed some coffee, and went upstairs to his bedroom. He showered. It was fine to be able to shower in his own home and enjoy the warmth of the water and soap his body down. After his shower, Roger put the clothes he slept in back on. He pulled on some white socks and a pair of black work shoes. Then he went back downstairs to wake Beth.

Roger shook Beth gently. "Rise and shine, Beth. Rise and shine, young lady."

Beth woke easily, rubbed her eyes, and sat up in the chair. "Oh, Roger. Good morning."

Roger smiled. "Good morning, Beth. Could you use some coffee?"

"Sure can."

"I have some brewed in the kitchen. Come on."

Roger and Beth walked to the kitchen, and Roger signaled to Beth to sit down. She did. Roger walked over to the cupboard, pulled out to ceramic coffee cups, and poured the coffee. "It'll have to be black," said Roger. "The cream must have long curdled."

"That's fine, Roger," said Beth.

Roger walked over to the table with the two mugs of coffee and placed one before Beth.

"You working today?" asked Roger.

"Yes. At seven. Breakfast and lunch today."

"Long day," said Roger, and he blew on his coffee.

"Yes, a long day."

"What day is it?"

"It's Saturday."

"Right. I kind of lost track of the days."

"I bet you have."

Roger took a sip of coffee. "Hot. It's great to have a cup of coffee."

"It sure is. Are you coming to breakfast at Mike's?"

"I'm not sure. I feel a little funny showing up all of a sudden after all this time away from home. People will have questions."

"Yes. People will have questions. It's the way Stonewall is. It's because people care for you in Stonewall."

"Yup."

"I care for you, too. You are a sweet man."

"That's debatable," Roger replied, and they both smiled.

"No. You are a sweet man, Roger Lee. And a kind man."

"But am I a man at all?"

"Yes, you are. The best kind of man."

"But I can't act fully as a man."

"You are still a man who acts like a man. Any man can have sex with a woman. It is easy to do. I have had sex with men who weren't manly, I am ashamed to say. Roger Lee, you are a man even if you can't do all the things that a man can do to a woman." Beth paused, not sure what to say and how to say it. She continued, "Roger. Dear Roger. I love you."

"Can you live your life as a celibate?"

"Yes."

Roger and Beth sipped their coffee in silence for a while. Roger finished his coffee and asked, "Can I get you some more coffee?" Roger walked over to the counter where the coffee maker sat, mug in his right hand.

"No. I better get going. Opening up for breakfast."

Beth finished her coffee and rose from the table. She walked over to a counter where her purse sat, and she grabbed it by the handles. She walked over to where Roger stood. He had poured himself more coffee, and the mug of coffee sat on the counter next to the coffee maker. She kissed him on his left cheek and said, "I love you." And she walked away and left the house and drove away.

Roger drove off twenty minutes later. It was nearly half past seven when Roger entered Mike's. There wasn't much of a crowd yet. Beth was taking an order from the Wolfords at a table toward the rear of Mike's, and Beth's back was to Roger when he entered the diner. To Roger's right, Bear Bailey sat at a window. He was eating a large portion of sausage gravy on a pancake. Bear turned his head to his left and looked up and saw Roger. He shot a large grin and stood.

"Welcome home," said Bear, and he gave Roger a strong, manly hug.

"Good to be back home," Roger replied.

ABOUT THE AUTHOR

 Derek Leaberry is sixty-two years of age. He was born in Washington, DC, and was raised in suburban Maryland. He graduated from Salisbury State College with a degree in history and has been married for thirty years. He and his wife have six children. Derek and his wife lived their first twenty-seven years of marriage on Maryland's Eastern Shore. They moved to Capon Bridge, West Virginia, a little over three years ago. They live on a twenty-eight-acre farm and raise chickens, ducks, geese, pigs, sheep, and goats. Derek is retired but previously worked in the printing industry for over thirty years. Previous to that, he worked in engineering and as a writer for the McLaughlin Group.

9 781662 488016